What if today never ends?

What if everything about life—everything anyone hoped to be, to do, to experience— never happens?

Whether sitting in a chair, driving down the road, in surgery, jumping off a cliff or flying ... that's where you'd be ... forever.

Unless ...

In One More Day, Erika Beebe, Marissa Halvorson, Kimberly Kay, J. Keller Ford, Danielle E. Shipley and Anna Simpson join L.S. Murphy to give us their twists, surprising us with answers to two big questions, all from the perspective of characters under the age of eighteen.

How do we restart time?

How do we make everything go back to normal?

The answers, in whatever the world—human, alien, medieval, fantasy or fairytale— could, maybe, happen today.

Right now.

What would you do if this happened ... to you?

One More Day

L.S. Murphy
with
Erika Beebe
Marissa Halvorson
Kimberly Kay
J. Keller Ford
Danielle E. Shipley
Anna Simpson

Kelsi,
Don't let anyone or anything
get in the way of your dreams.
Go for it.
Erika Beebe

J. Taylor Publishing

ONE MORE DAY

Published by J. Taylor Publishing
www.jtaylorpublishing.com

ISBN 978-1-937744-37-3

First Printing: December 2013

To all, young and old, enjoy your 'one more day'.

Time Piece

Anna Simpson

J. Taylor Publishing

It's ten P.M. on Saturday, and I'm holding Bradley Warren McCurry's surprisingly dry, warm hand. Every step closer to my front door means saying good-bye, and it's getting harder and harder to breathe.

Is he going to kiss me? Should I kiss him?

I've waited for this moment. A moment that thrives in my heart and dreams but never seemed possible. Yet, here we are. Together.

His thumb strokes my hand as we come to my front gate. Brad slips between the gate and me, and opens the latch. We walk through and stand face to face in the golden glow of the streetlamp. I can count each long lash around his green eyes and every crease in his lips. Small droplets cling to his light-ash hair, and his Adam's apple rises and falls as he swallows. He's like a magnet drawing me forward.

Stepping back, he stumbles and grabs me for balance.

We move together like dancers in slow motion, Brad pulling me to him and my chest touching his for a heartbeat. He steps aside, again taking me with him, and I spin within his arms and fall against his toned body.

I tingle everywhere we touch. This is the most wonderful thing that has ever happened. My dreams were never this good.

You can do this, Sadie.

I reach up, rest my hand on his shoulder, and stretch on my tippy-toes.

Lips to lips. Just do it.

His eyes are half closed with a radiant blush on his cheeks. His lips are moist with the tip of his tongue barely visible. He has never looked more gorgeous, or still, reminding me of a wax figure.

Closer still … millimeters away, I realize, he's not breathing.

Not moving.

Doing nothing but standing there.

"Brad?"

Nothing.

Behind and to the left, something moves in the shadows. I step away, my heart in my throat, not understanding any of this, and rub my eyes.

"I can't believe this," I say, grabbing for Brad's arm. My fist closes on empty air. I spin, taking in my yard and the street behind me. He's gone.

Something snaps inside me.

Bend with it, Sadie. Bend with it, or break.

"Sadie?"

That voice!

Turning toward the shadows, I wait. A girl steps into the golden light. Not just any girl. I find my own face peering back at me from the dimness. Hers is not an exact copy of mine; it's older with dark circles under brandy-brown eyes. Long stringy hair hangs down to her elbows. An oversized burnt-orange sweater hangs on her thin shoulders.

My eyes go wide as I cover my mouth to stop from screaming.

The stranger shivers, taking an unsure step closer to me.

My knees give out. I land hard on the grass and dig my

fingers deep into the patchy lawn, needing something to hold on to. The coolness of it feels good. Real.

"Joe needs our help." The girl rushes over, dropping to her knees beside me. The icy chill of loss and fear reminds me of when Uncle Joe showed up at our doorstep four years ago.

I push myself along the ground to give me some distance from her. I don't know if it's because she looks like me, or because of Brad's disappearance, or her mentioning Uncle Joe, but I'm freaking out inside.

She reaches out a trembling hand but stops before touching me. "Help me. I can't do this alone. Believe me, I've tried. You know the machine Joe's been working on?"

I don't know; I'm not up-to-date on his latest project.

"It works. I mean you can turn it on, and it does stuff, but not the stuff he intended it to do." Two fat tears slide down her sunken cheeks, and cling to her chin. There are lines in her face. How old is she?

I swallow, and nod. "What's turned on?" I ask in a whisper.

"A friggin' time machine." Adie uses her filthy sweater to wipe her face. "I saw Joe get hurt tonight. Horrible ... it was horrible."

What? What's she saying? "Uncle Joe is hurt? Time machine? Who are you? Where is Brad?"

"He calls me Adie, but we don't have time for this."

"I don't understand." Closing my eyes, I count to five. This has to be a dream, a nightmare. It can't be real. It can't.

Adie sighs. "Joe built a time machine. He did it! And when I mean did *it*, I mean he screwed the whole human race. Time is stuck in a loop which is getting shorter and shorter." Adie hiccups. "And the freaks in the black suits keep coming. I can't bear to do it again—not alone."

"Do what? What do you have to do? Where's Brad? Where's

Uncle Joe?"

"We have to destroy it!" Adie stands. "Before they hurt Joe."

My heart skips a beat. No. I can't lose him, too. I'd have no one. I choke on a sob. "Who's going to hurt Uncle Joe?"

"His financiers." Adie grabs my arm and pulls me up. "We're not safe here. We really need to go."

Looking up at my own face makes me feel queasy. This is too much. "What if Brad calls?"

"Brad's fine." Adie holds eye contact with me and frowns.

My phone needs a charge, too, but I get the feeling if I tell her that, she's going to lose it.

"Look. Like I said, Joe made a time machine. People want it. They think it works. And they think, with Joe out of the way, all they need to do is take it. Oh, and get rid of loose ends."

This isn't good. "Loose ends?" Butterflies fly through my stomach and work their way up my throat.

"Oh, yeah, sorry. They think you're me." Adie stares at her feet.

I blow out a long breath. "You're kidding, right?" She's got to be. This is some kind of sick joke. Please, let it be a joke.

"Are you serious? Look at me." Adie spreads her arms and hands wide. "Who do you think I am?"

"Well … you look a little like me, so what?" I swallow, choking on something hard and cold that might be truth.

"Quit being such an ass. Come on." She yanks me forward.

I'm not an ass, and if Uncle Joe is hurt, I know I'll help her, but first I've got to verify her story. "So, Unc is at the lab?" I withdraw my phone from my jean pocket. My hands are shaking as I try to hit Unc's number.

"No, but the machine is." Adie stops and turns. "Brilliant. Give me your phone." She punches in Brad's number, and begins pacing.

Part of me wants to tear the phone from her hands, and the other side is relieved. Four trips to the porch and back, and she says, "Hey, get up ... it's about eleven. Why ..."

Brad's at home asleep.

She's not talking to him like that, is she?

"Funny. Get your butt out of bed, and get over here ... Yes, I mean drive. Friggin' steal it. There may be no tomorrow, anyway."

Oh, my god, she called Brad. She called Brad, and now there's no hope for me, for us! The trees rustle above my head, and I jump. Faces appear in every shadow, and I hear sounds I can't explain.

Brad's mom's mini SUV stops beside me as I stumble toward the street.

That was fast. I pull the handle several times. Didn't he just leave? What is happening here?

"Unlock the door," Adie says.

The lock releases, and I jump in the front seat.

He looks real enough.

Adie climbs in the back, pushing a large sports bag aside. "Omigosh, clean your car much."

Brad's head moves back and forth, his gaze landing on me, Adie, me, and Adie again.

Air catches in my throat as he glances at the backseat. "Adie, Brad. Brad, Adie," I say.

Brad blushes as Adie meets his gaze. I want to vomit. Instead, I finger comb my hair. We might look alike, but Adie's a mess.

"Holy crap. I didn't know you were twins." Brad frowns, and I cross my arms over my chest, feeling a fool. "Yeah, we don't talk about it much." It's all I can think to say.

"Why not? It's so cool," he says.

"Don't even think about it, stud," Adie says.

I cringe, my face burning.

Adie settles in the back seat, shaking her head. "Brad, go to Fourth and Lex."

"Sure." Brad faces toward his wing mirror and spins in a two-point turn. "Can I ask why?"

"You can ask." Adie says.

Far off somewhere, sirens sound. I glance up and around the car, seeking the source. As the sirens get closer, I grip my knees and push myself back into the seat. With each breath, they come closer, following us, gaining on us. Flashing lights are far behind us, and Brad pulls over. My throat tightens as I swivel to look out the back window and find Adie's face is as pale as I am on the inside.

The rear window fills with white, blue, white … blue, white. The strobe draws me into a memory of Uncle Joe standing in a doorway soaked to the skin. He'd been crying when he came in and grabbed me so hard, shaking against me, whispering between sobs.

That night was the first time I had ever seen a grown man cry.

A police car and ambulance pass us. Brad follows them. They get farther and farther ahead, smaller and smaller in the distance. As we come up to Fourth and Lex, I choke, undo my seatbelt, grab the dashboard, and lean against the cold glass.

Uncle Joe's car has T-boned a white van.

No!

Two men in dark suits sit on the curb. A paramedic holds an icepack to the forehead of the smaller of the two.

Adie's hand clenches my shoulder. Her breath comes in stuttering gasps. I stare harder at the car.

Uncle Joe didn't just run the stop sign. From the damage— collapsed front end, bending the van like an arrowhead—Unc had to be speeding.

But he wouldn't do that. Not after Mom and Dad's accident.

Unc's front window has a large hole on the driver's side. A lumpy blanket lies on the hood of his car, a brown loafer peeking out.

No seatbelt? Why?

Adie's touch is gone. I close my eyes and lean back in my seat. My head spins. I reach up, needing something to steady me. Something solid. Something strong.

Warmth under my palm tells me I'm no longer in the car. My hand is on Brad's shoulder. I'm standing in my front yard, staring up at him.

"Omigod." My knees give out, and I land hard on the grass. Where's the accident?

"We don't have time for this," Adie says, coming out of the dimness.

What the— "Uncle Joe! We've got to help him." I scramble to my feet.

Adie blinks. "Right, yes. Give me your phone." She takes it from my outstretched hand and punches in Brad's number, pacing again. Like before. Before?

"Hey, get up … it's about eleven. Why …"

She's not talking to Brad like that, is she?

"Funny. Get your butt out of bed, and get over here … Yes, I mean drive. Friggin' steal it. There may be no tomorrow, anyway."

Oh, my god, she called Brad. She called Brad! He can help us get to Uncle Joe. I stumble toward the street. The trees rustle above my head, and I wipe my tears away, imaging Uncle Joe's face in every shadow. I grab for Adie's hand, and hold tight as Brad drives around the corner.

Dancing on my toes, I pull on the handle several times, sure

we can prevent the accident. "Unlock the door." The lock releases, and I jump in the front seat. "Adie, Brad. Brad, Adie."

Adie climbs in the back, pushing a large sports bag aside.
"Yeah, I know. Wow, we're twins."

A gasp catches in my throat as he glances toward the backseat. Brad blushes. Immediately, my cheeks burn.

"Fourth and Lex, and hurry. We need to get there before
you hear sirens."

"What? Can I ask why?" Brad faces his wing mirror, and
does a two-point turn.

Uncle Joe. We have to help Uncle Joe.

"You can ask." Adie's foot taps nervously against the back
of my seat.

As we travel to our destination, Brad turns up the radio and
sings along. My heart pounds in my chest, and I glare at him.
He's taking forever.

When we get to the intersection, the street is empty. Hands
on the glass, I stare out at the four-way stop in the middle of
a sleepy residential area. Where's Uncle Joe?

"Stop now, or go through it and park, so we can double
back," Adie says.

Is she afraid the accident will happen right on top of us? Did
it already happen? What is going on?

"No one is here." I scan the older homes through the back
window. "There aren't even lights on in any of the houses."

Adie takes a deep breath, and when she exhales, her breathing is loud and stuttery. Brad stops and she jumps out. Staying
away from the cones of light, she nears the center of the intersection.

Brad turns down the radio and faces the back window. "Why
did we have to stop here?" Together, we watch Adie circling the
road, face tilted toward the road as if looking for something.

"I'm not sure." I smile weakly at Brad and get out of the car. Before walking away, I say, "We'll be right back."

Adie stands where the accident had happened, kicking at invisible objects and mumbling. The closer I get, the clearer her words are. "It must be here ... must be."

"What are you looking for?" There is nothing on the ground.

"A key—"

"Try this." I remove a mini flashlight that I use as a zipper pull from my hoody. "Sweep it over the area."

My gaze follows the oblong circle of light she aims at the pavement. We find small glass shards scattered across the area, each catching the light like discarded diamonds.

So, there was an accident.

Not far from the broken glass, the street has an obvious stain by the sidewalk, a trail of dark droplets abruptly ending in the center. "Adie, is that blood?" An image of the injured man with an ice pack to his head comes to mind.

"Could be. Each timeline is slightly different."

Timeline. The word bounces around in my mind for a moment. A rush of fear bubbles up, and I push it away. If that's blood from the man from the van, Unc could be fine. This is good news.

"What was that?" I ask.

"What?"

"Back up the light." I walk over and pick up what I thought was a large coin. My lips tremble as the chain of Uncle Joe's pocket watch swings from my fingertips. "It's Unc's watch."

"Okay. Good. We can go to the lab." Adie's shoulders relax. She pinches the chain and pulls it from my palm as she leads the way back to the car.

I spin slowly in the darkness. Arms take hold of me. I rise up on tippy-toes facing skyward, reaching for Brad's lips with my own.

"Omigod." It's happened again. I force myself to breathe. My fingers tighten on his sleeve.

Behind Brad, Adie moves by the house. She raises her fist, and gives me a thumbs up. My eyes go wide as I cover my mouth to stop from swearing aloud. Before I do or say anything, Brad is gone.

"I can't believe it." How many times am I going to do this?

"Sadie." Adie smiles wide, the chain of Unc's pocket watch swinging from her fingertips.

"I don't understand." I lose my balance and land hard on the grass.

"I think we're getting ahead of it." Adie's narrow hips wiggle back and forth in a happy dance.

"Ahead of what, exactly? And why does the watch matter so much?" I still don't get it. It's an old pocket watch that probably keeps crappie time. So, who cares? We just have to find Uncle Joe.

She reaches out a hand, letting the golden watch swing in my face. "It's the key to—" She jumps and glances behind her.

I follow her gaze, but the street is empty.

Adie brings her sleeve to her shining face and inhales deeply. "We gotta get going! Keep your eyes open for a white van."

"Right." I put my feet under me as start to rise. "You mean like the one in the accident."

"Don't be stupid! That was no accident." Adie snaps her fingers under my nose. "Give me your phone."

I slap her hand away. I know what I have to do, and dial Brad's number.

"Sadie?" His voice is sleepy.

"Yep, it's me." I stop, and cough to clear my throat. "I need you to give me a ride."

"What time it is?" Brad exhales, making a static noise through the phone.

"It's about eleven. I wouldn't ask, but it's important." A quick glance at my wristwatch.

Adie grabs the phone. "Hey, get up! Get your butt out of bed, and get over here. Yes, I mean drive. Friggin' steal it." She holds out the phone.

I snatch it back and march towards the street, ignoring the trees rustling above my head. This time, the shadows are only shadows, and the sounds of the night only noises of nature. Adie joins me at the roadside.

Brad stops the SUV beside us.

I pull on the handle several times, ready to get going. The lock releases, and I jump in the front seat. "Adie, Brad. Brad, Adie."

She climbs in the back, pushing the large sports bag aside.

Brad blushes, once again meeting her gaze.

"Yeah, we're twins get over it," I say this time, expecting him to be upset.

He smiles wide like he likes being here. "This is so cool."

"Don't even think about it, stud." Adie clicks her seatbelt in place. "Brad, go to Hastings and Abbot."

"Sure. Can I ask why?" Brad faces his wing mirror, and does yet another two-point turn.

"You can ask." Adie leans back in her seat, gazing out the window, still clutching the watch.

"To the lab." Brad turns down the radio. "Will your Uncle be there?"

"Might be." I stare at my hands and play with a cuticle.

"Then what are we doing?" Brad turns his head a little, checking his mirrors.

"We have to pick up a package." Adie mumbles.

Nodding, Brad turns up the radio so loud we can't talk. Grateful to end the awkward conversation, and because I hate lying, Adie seems more than fine with it. I close my eyes, leaning one way or another with the cars momentum as Brad drives.

The car slows, I open my eyes, and my uncle's building comes into view.

"We're here already?" I stretch as we drive pass the two-story, medical-clinic-like building. Anything could be in there. As Brad circles the block searching for a good place to park, I'm on full alert looking for a white van.

"You going to be very long?" Brad picks a spot in the no-parking zone.

"Should only be a sec," I say, wondering if he knows I'm not telling the truth.

"Back in a shake." Adie opens her door. "Let's go."

"Right." Face burning, I get out, too, as a white van turns the corner toward us. I point at it. "What's—"

"It's them." Adie ducks.

I freeze and stare as a delivery man dressed in a blue uniform drives by. *Express Delivery* is printed in black, red, and yellow across its sliding door.

"What wrong with you? Next time, don't stand there like a big, friggin' idiot. Let's get going." Adie turns and runs toward the back of the building.

I can't help but glance at Brad. Before he can ask me what's wrong, I run after Adie, following her down the lane to the loading bay and the employee's entrance. She holds the watch up, and the lock clicks. Giving the heavy door a push makes it silently open.

Adie clutches my arm. "There is something I need to tell you."

"Now? You just said we needed to hurry." I want to scream—afraid of starting another loop.

"This can't wait. Brad's going to die tonight."

I slide from her grip, slowly spinning away.

Stretching tall, reaching high, I hold tight to Brad's shoulder. I keep my eyes closed and pull him close. As I tighten my grip, he becomes less and less solid until there is nothing to hold on to.

I sob.

"What kind of person are you?" I drop to my knees defeated. "Brad is going to die." I can't do this anymore. Not to him.

"Call him."

"No." I bring out my phone from my pocket. Adie grabs my hand before I can throw it into the street. "I won't let Brad die! It's not right. We need to warn him."

"He needs to give us a lift." She reaches for me. "We're not the bad guys here."

I don't believe her. Trading one life for another is not okay. "You're sick." I shake my head. "Something is seriously wrong with you."

"Do you really think I would do this, if I could avoid it?" Perspiration glitters gold on her skin. "What do you think happened to make me—us—do this? Think about it."

I can't think and shake my head.

"Joe believed that, with the machine destroyed, time would reset." She punches in Brad's number and begins pacing. "I happen to believe him."

"Pretty convenient."

Adie rakes her hair as she walks toward the porch. "Believe, or don't. We still need to do the same thing. I never thought it'd come to this." Far away beyond my cloud of confusion, Adie says, "Hey, get up … it's about eleven. Why? Funny, get your

butt out of bed, and get over here. Yes, I mean drive. Friggin'
steal it. There may be no tomorrow, anyway."

No tomorrow? She's going to do this, no matter what. I
stumble toward the street. The trees rustle above my head. The
varying shadows blur behind my tears. I push my fists hard
into my hoody pockets and wait until Brad drives around the
corner. Somehow, this has to stop.

"Unlock the door." Adie pulls on the handle, pushing me
toward the back. "Brad, I'm Adie."

I climb in, pulling the large soft sports bag to my lap. A gasp
catches in my throat as he glances at me. I quickly wipe my
eyes, my stomach knotting up.

"Holly crap—" Brad's gaze jumps from me to Adie, and
back again.

I stare into the darkness, and crush the bag to my chest like
a teddy bear. The pleasant scent of fresh laundered clothing
puffs into the air.

"Don't take this the wrong way, Brad, but shut it," Adie says.

"But it's so cool," he says.

Adie shakes her head, and stares out the front window. "We
need to get to Hastings and Abbot as quick as you can."

"Sure. Can I ask why?" Brad faces his wing mirror, and pulls
a two-point turn.

"You can ask." Adie leans back in her seat.

"Okay." He taps his thigh in time with the music.

I tighten my grip on my makeshift teddy bear, biting my lip.

"What are we doing?" Brad asks.

"We have to pick up a package." Adie turns up the radio so
loud we can't talk.

Grateful, I close my eyes. Leaning one way or another as
the car shifts, we drive to the lab. I need to think and to figure
out a way to stop this.

The car slows. We drive past the lab, a two-story, medical-clinic-like building. They could be in there waiting for us.

Brad circles the block. "You going to be very long?" He pulls up into a no-parking zone in the loading bay.

"Should only take a sec," I say, wondering if he can tell I'm lying.

"Do you mind staying in the car?" Adie asks, opening her door. "Let's go." She doesn't wait for an answer.

I get out, too, and run after Adie, following her up the loading bay stairs and to the employee's entrance.

She holds the heavy door open as I catch up and clutches my arm. "I'm sorry about Brad."

I clench my jaw, ignoring her; yanking my arm free, I walk on.

"Let's hope time resets," she says.

I can't hope, and won't believe her last ditch effort to trick me. What if I listen to her? What if I live, but Brad doesn't. What kind of person does it make me?

Once inside, I take the stairs, two at a time like in gym class. I'm puffing by the time I make it to the lab door.

Adie comes up behind me, and we go in.

The motion-sensitive lamps turn on, and the office fills with bright white light. Banks of servers line one wall, their LED lights changing to a different pattern with each flash. The plain room has an open console in the corner between the door and a bank of servers. Large cables feed the workstation—the complicated control panel would be just as comfortable in a commercial aircraft.

Kitty-corner to the console, and taking up the rest of the space in the room, is an enlarged snow globe. Small particles float inside the glass like a sparkle and soap-flake blizzard. A large dentist's chair sits in the center of the storm on a raised podium. The particles dance around the base, and swirl up through the air, as if controlled by a constant wind current.

What are the particles made of? I glance at Adie. She shivers. My heart picks up the pace, and a slick coating of cold perspiration covers my paling skin. That couldn't be Uncle Joe? "What are those things floating in the glass?" I ask.

"Find me something heavy and solid, Sadie." She doesn't answer my question.

It dawns on me, the faster we get this done, the safer Brad is. Out by the stairs are a couple of fire extinguishers. I carry them back, leaving one by the console and dropping the second extinguisher inside the door. Just in case.

A metal and vinyl visitor's chair tucks under the doorknob easily.

Watching the door, I back up, bumping the console. Unc's watch sits in a small slot under the LCD screen. Adie leans over the workstation, her gaze on the flashing buttons, fingers on the keyboard. I come up to her side as she logs in. The overhead light shudders and grows dark. The lights on the console and the super computer do, too. A moment passes in silence. The room flares to life with the whirring of hard drives, the clicking of the storm against the glass within the snow globe, and flashing of LED lamps filling the room.

A window on the screen displays a countdown. "What are you doing?" I draw her away from the keyboard. "We are destroying it, right?"

"Yes." Adie picks up the fire extinguisher by the door, and tosses up and down to test its weight. She swallows hard. "Turn the screen. I need to see when it hits zero."

"Why?" I know why.

She stares at me. "There's only one way. I have to do it from … from the inside."

"What? What are you saying?" I glance over at the time machine. If this doesn't work, I could be facing the next loop completely alone.

"Don't think about it." She smiles sadly. "Hang in there. I just need a few minutes." Her gaze falls over my shoulder, a chill crawls up my back, and I turn toward the door.

Brad's face pushes against the narrow wired window, his distorted face smearing blood against the glass, while a gun barrel presses into his temple. A man's dark suit shadows him.

"Let them in," Adie says.

I run to the window. Gently reaching for Brad's cheek, I touch the glass. *You can do this. You can. No one has to die.*

Adie cradles the fire extinguisher and marches toward the globe. "They don't know there are two of us. Keep it that way, and we'll finish this thing."

Right. I grab the chair and tug. To my surprise, it doesn't budge.

"Good. Pretend you're having trouble with door," she says.

"I don't need to pretend." All I can see is Brad's battered face. I'm already blocking the window, pulling and pushing madly at the chair. Still nothing. Tears fall as I fight to get it free; my sweaty palm slips, and I bash my knee.

The door to the globe opens with a whisper. A stream of whirling, cold air momentarily fills the room. More determined than ever, I struggle with the chair.

"Do you want him to die? Let us in ... now." The stranger's accent scares me to the core, and when he presses the gun to Brad's head, I tug harder at the legs of the chair.

My makeshift barrier gives way as Adie crashes around inside the globe. Flashes and sparks explode within the device. She shrieks as the fire extinguisher melts into a puddle by the pedestal. White gas bellows in the center and gathers in a cloud.

I suck in my breath and scream.

Brad bursts into the room and pushes me aside as the gun-man comes at me with his arm raised. Brad jumps him, the gun falls, circling and sliding away from a tangle of arms and legs. He breaks free long enough to bring down one of his fists on the man's face.

A loud explosion knocks me to my knees. I fall forward and reach for Brad as sparkles and flakes swirl around us. Some of the particles pass right through me—as cold as ghosts.

A second man shouts at me, but I don't understand a word he says. He grabs me by the scruff of my hoody and drags me to the corner console, where he throws me onto the desk and points at random buttons. I use the mouse, trying to bring up a window, but the screen freezes. He grabs my hair, yanking me off my feet, and I tumble to the floor and roll.

The giant snow globe hovers off the ground, spinning. Adie's body drags along the inside. Her scream rises in octaves until it becomes a whistle of wind. Each time around, she becomes more of a blur. Fabric and skin smears the surface of the globe, fragmenting, spinning, and fading into smaller and smaller puzzle pieces.

I can't bear to watch, and turn away, putting my hands over my ears.

Brad rushes to me as the first man goes for his gun. Unable to say a word, I point at it. The gunman raises his arm, taking aim, and the sound that follows is louder than anything I've ever experienced—ear ringing, scream inducing, loud.

Brad stands like a statue—the only thing changing is the blossom of deep red spreading across his chest. As shock re-leases him, he crumbles.

No!

I pick up the abandoned fire extinguisher. As heavy as it is,

I'm able to raise it over my head and let it fly at the gunman. Not waiting, I push the second man into the console. Instead of grabbing me, he huffs as he hits the desk edge.

At Brad's side, I drop to my knees. He's too heavy to lift, so all I can do is straighten his legs. I snuggle in, trying to wrap one of his arms around me, but it slides off. I try again. This time, I hold on tight, pulling it into place, imaging he's holding me. One long shallow breath ruffles my hair.

It's time to spin. To go back to my front yard to watch Adie come out of the dimness with a new plan of attack. To find a way to avoid this moment yet again. To remember what happened and work around it.

Instead, a new sensation overtakes me. Each moment is an effort, as if I'm trying to breath underwater. The swirling storm above my head slows down and gathers together, becoming a miniature of the Milky Way. The wait between each breath seems an eternity.

An incredible effort is necessary to move my heavy hand an inch across Brad's still chest. Above me the particles stop in midair.

It's not just the particles. Everything stops.

No! I'm supposed to go back! To start over!

I can't breathe.

The lights dim; I know I'm dying and accept my failure. I've lost. Brad's dead. Adie's dead. Unc's dead. It's over, but not the way Adie hoped.

Lost in the darkness, I close my eyes. Brad's thumb slowly strokes my hand. Grief and relief tear me in two. He's not gone, yet.

With each stroke, I can see a little more until I'm aware of my new surroundings. Where are we?

Brad slips between the gate and me. He unlatches it,

but holds it closed, facing me under the golden glow of the streetlamp. I take in each long lash around his green eyes, and every crease in his lips. The droplets in his light-ash hair, and his Adam's apple rising and falling as he swallows, reminds me of everything I lost only moments ago.

I move forward. He steps back, hitting the gate. It opens, and he stumbles, grabbing my hand for balance.

My chest touches his for a long, slow heartbeat. He steps again back, taking me with him.

I pull him closer, resting my other hand on his shoulder, and stretch on my tippy-toes. Not wanting to wait another second. Daring Adie at any moment to steal away my kiss.

Next time, I'll find a way to save you.

Brad sucks in his breath. He leans down, cupping my hair. His strong solid arm gently lifts me up off my feet. I wrap my arms around his neck, intending to never let go, and he closes the last millimetre of space between us. Our lips meet—so soft, sweet and gentle. A rush of joy fills me to bursting.

When Brad drops me to the ground, tears cling to my lashes. Afraid he'll disappear, I clutch his sleeve.

His eyes half-close, and there's a radiant blush on his cheeks as he gazes at me. His lips are moist with the tip of his tongue barely visible. He has never looked more alive. Behind him and to the left, something moves in the shadows of my house.

I step away, my heart in my throat.

Unc ambles out. "Sadie, it's time to come in."

No Adie.

"I'll call you tomorrow." Brad returns to the gate, sliding his hands into his jean pockets. As he gets in his car, he glances at me, and I finger wave.

"Are you busy tomorrow?" Uncle Joe asks. "After reading your physics paper, I think you need to spend some time in the lab." He drapes a protective arm around my shoulders, guiding me to the porch. "I've got these new investors—"

"Stop right there." I smile, resting my head on his sweater vest."Unc, we need to talk."

Acknowledgements

For my son, Bossman.

I'd like to thank the Sisterhood of the Travelling Pens at Scribophile.com. Their attitudes, and supportive feedback molded me into the writer that I am today.

Anna Simpson

Anna Simpson, mother of Bossman, enjoys living the good life near the US-Canadian border, in beautiful British Columbia. You will have better luck Googling Emaginette than her given name. Anna chose a web persona that would standout; so far it's one of a kind.

Dark Rose

Marissa Halvorson

J. Taylor Publishing

A boom shook the classroom. Scarlett shrieked, and clapped a hand over her mouth. Heart slamming in her chest, she lifted her eyes and scanned the room. In one corner, Matthew stared straight ahead of him. Behind him, Bailey leaned so far over her desk, Scarlett thought she would fall headfirst off the table.

A few desks in front of Scarlett, Jed pushed his exam away from him, his glasses sliding halfway off his nose. He crossed his arms and leaned back in his seat. Leah tapped her pen against the desk without rhythm, fluttering her eyes at Toby.

The rumble didn't seem to affect anyone.

How did they miss that? There had been a noise. *Hadn't there?*

The stress of the test must have been getting to Scarlett. She shook her head, as if to rid herself of the confusion, and forced her gaze back to the paper in front of her. The instructions at the top read: In no less than 500 words, persuade a fellow student to part with his or her most valuable possession or deepest desire for the greater good.

With pencil to page, she began to write, only to glance at her watch—twenty minutes left in the exam, and half her essay remained undone. No wonder she was nervous.

A second boom rocked the schoolroom, and she gripped the shaking desk.

Nobody else did the same.

This can't be real. I'm going crazy, or something. Maybe I'm dreaming. She squeezed her eyes shut, inhaled, exhaled, and returned to her paper. She pressed her pencil against the page and stifled a curse when the lead broke. Reaching for her sharpener, she clutched the writing utensil as the classroom shook for the third time. The essay vibrated off her desk, the nearly blank composition fluttering in a breeze to the ground.

What the hell? Her imagination had not pushed her test off the table. It was capable of a lot of things but not that.

Scarlett waited for the rumble to happen again. The clock ticked behind her. Fifteen minutes. Twelve. Ten. She'd never finish the assessment. How could she focus when the room kept shaking? Scarlett retrieved and set her paper on the desk, and leaned back in her chair, staring at the mostly blank page.

The boom came right then.

"Holy shit!" She turned and eyed Leah, who sat right next to her. The other girl didn't look at her. In fact, nobody did. Mr. Krilling didn't scold her for her outburst. *What the heck?* She gripped the table, and stared at the clock which dangled at a precarious angle. *It's only ten-thirty?* Hadn't it read 10:52 seconds ago? She'd been watching the time, waiting for it to disappear before she finished the essay. *Earthquakes, time changes and people ignoring me? This can't be my imagination.*

Scarlett stood and walked to the front. Standing in front of her unmoving teacher, she poked Mr. Krilling's shoulder. He didn't respond.

"Hey," she said, hoping someone would make an annoyed sound or tell her to shut up. Anything to say they knew she stood before them.

Nothing happened.

She fled the room without another glance. Stopping outside the door, Scarlett glanced down the hall. Finding it empty, she ran to the right, feet slapping against the tile floors, and peeked into classrooms as she passed them. Some teachers stood at their boards, but nobody lifted their gazes. She rounded a corner, almost sliding into the far wall, and hit the double doors to the outside. She pushed them open and froze.

Outside, the ground shook continually, and Scarlett bent her legs to keep her balance.

People ran screaming in every direction.

Huge, metal beasts, like dogs with razor sharp teeth and claws, bounded past, chasing groups of people as if they were swarms of mice.

Storm clouds darkened the sky, but no rain fell. In the center of the mess, a figure in a dark cloak stood, arms spread wide. Its body shook with what Scarlett thought must be laughter, although she couldn't hear over all the screaming.

Scarlett, herself, stood frozen. *So my imagination is acting up.* She glanced back at the doors through which she'd come.

The whole school had disappeared, replaced with a park, surrounded by a few benches.

What the—

"Hey! Why are you just standing? Do something!" a girl's voice said.

Scarlett jumped. Something touched her arm, and everything stopped. Or seemed to, anyway. Noise disappeared, but everyone kept moving. She spun toward the grip.

The owner of the hand on her arm was a girl about Scarlett's age, her eyes shimmering a dark blue, black hair a contrast to Scarlett's blonde. "How come you're not helping with the plan?" she asked. The girl's grip tightened around Scarlett's arm, her brow deepening into a scowl. With her curly tresses and mascara-lined eyelashes, she seemed like one of the preppy girls from school.

Wait! What plan?

A dog-beast bounded past before Scarlett could ask the question. A girl, whose mouth stretched wide in a scream, sprinted in the same direction, chased by the beast.

Preppy-girl stared toward the woman who disappeared in less than a second. In the same amount of time, she came through again, mouth open in that same scream and disappeared just as fast once more.

A woman tripped and fell. She stood again and tripped and fell.

A huge man lifted one of the beasts and threw it once, twice, a third time, just like the girl. There, then not. There, then not.

"What's going on?" Scarlett whirled and stumbled away as the vanishing girl came through again in her line of sight.

Preppy's mouth opened wide, gaze toward the repeating people. "Oh, my god! Everyone's doing it like they're—they're stuck in time."

"Or something," Scarlett said. Though, time seemed right, somehow. *Trapped in time ...* Could things get any weirder?

Scarlett spun to face Preppy. Until they'd touched, everything was fine—or, well, at least not stuck. "Who are you?"

The dark-haired girl flipped her hair over her shoulder and blinked her heavily penciled eyelids at Scarlett. "Excuse me? Who am *I?* You're the one who waltzed in here and acted like you didn't have a clue what was going on."

"I *don't.*" She threw her arms up. "I-I was writing an exam when this random shaking happened, and the time went back in my class, and people just stopped. Then I came out here to this. How am I supposed to know?" She let out a breath. *Calm down, Scarlett. You need to think, and you can't when you're freaking out.*

Preppy gazed through narrowed eyes toward Scarlett. "You're

obviously not from around here. What's your name, stranger?"

"Scarlett, but that's—"

"Look over where the cloaked guy . . ." The girl trailed off.

Scarlett only had time to see a cloak disappear. People continued to show up and leave, repeating their actions. She moved to stand in the place the figure had been in and glanced around. Nearly every corner of the square was visible from her position. "Who was that?" she asked, turning in a circle.

Preppy pulled her pink sweater tighter around her shoulders, rolling her eyes. "You're out of the loop, aren't you? That's the Dark Rose. Trying to destroy the world? Setting the apocalypse into motion? Any of this sound familiar?"

After the word 'destroy', nothing registered with Scarlett. "What do you mean, destroying our world? When did this start?"

Preppy popped a piece of gum and chomped, not bothering to keep her mouth closed. All the craziness around them, and the girl chewed gum like it all happened every day. After several minutes of gum squishing between teeth, Preppy said, "Couple days ago. We need to find the Dark Rose, though. I have a bad feeling about him going poof."

Scarlett backed away a few steps, shaking her head. *I'm sorry, but this is ridiculous. The Dark Rose destroying the world?* "None of this makes any sense. This has to be a dream. I fell asleep in my exam and somehow ended up here."

Preppy wrapped her hand around Scarlett's arm, manicured nails digging into skin and making Scarlett wince. "You can leave if you want, but you won't find a way to reverse time unless you help me," she said.

Vision flickering, Scarlett yanked away. For a moment, she stood in a square empty of people except for one. A dark figure in a cloak stood at the center of everything, his hands spread wide. From an alley stepped one of the dog-beasts. Followed by another, and followed by three more.

She jerked back to herself and twirled in a circle, but the only real person in the square with her was Preppy. "What happened?"

Preppy's eyes widened before she blinked and gazed at Scarlett, "The Dark Rose."

Right, whatever. It was too weird. "Who are you?"

"My name's Letta," she said.

Scarlett frowned. *Why does she seem so familiar to me?* Her hair fell past her shoulders, with waves almost exactly the same as Scarlett's. The only difference was the color. Even their eyes were the same shape. She reached out and touched Letta's shoulder. Her vision shifted and she saw herself, as if from the other girl's eyes. She flinched and shook her head.

"Parallel universes," Letta said.

Scarlett swallowed. "Is that ... possible?"

"Didn't you feel it? We're probably copies of each other, or something."

A soon as Scarlett tried to think through the idea, she blanked. It wasn't possible. A parallel universe? That girl, Letta, was her? '*Also*', an unknown voice in her head said, '*your universes have touched. You're intermingling right now.*'

"Intermingle ..." Scarlett closed her eyes.

"You heard that, didn't you?"

"Um ..."

"You're not imagining anything. If you're hallucinating, I am too, and I *am not crazy.* Our worlds are intermingling—that has to be what's happening."

Scarlett sighed. She might as well go along with the silly dream. Once she figured out how to get out of her predicament, she'd probably wake up. "How do we separate them?"

"I—oh" Letta stopped, eyes glazing over. She whirled, and Scarlett followed her gaze just in time to catch a glimpse of a flash of black disappearing around a corner. Letta grabbed Scarlett by the wrist. "Come on. This way—I think I saw him."

They sprinted in the direction of the vanishing black, darting down the alley. "Where are we going?" Scarlett asked between gasps of air.

Letta twirled the bracelet on her wrist. "Down here."

"We need to figure out how to separate our worlds!"

They skidded to a halt. A low almost-squeal emanated from Letta's mouth for a few seconds before she let out a huge breath. "Here's what I think: we locate the Dark Rose; we'll find our answers." She gestured in the direction the black had disappeared.

Scarlett gripped the girl's shoulder. "Why did our universes converge? Did we touch each other and cause them to intermingle?"

"I don't know!" Letta threw her arms up and stalked down the alley. "This is science." She shuddered. "Science makes me sick."

Scarlett followed at a jog and bit her lip. "What were you doing before?"

Letta turned a corner, and Scarlett swerved to follow her. "I was . . . I was working on a strategy to destroy the Dark Rose."

"So you were focused on a plan. I was concentrating on my exam. I can draw two theories. One—"

"Would you *shut up?*" Letta veered around another corner. "None of this is going to help us. What we need is to search for him. I'm sure we'll find answers then."

"He wants to demolish the world! We need to separate them, not let him kill us." Scarlett moved to stand in front of the other girl. "There has to be a simple way to . . . to . . . ."

"To what?"

Lowering her gaze, Scarlett said, "Well, if we eliminate the connection between us, there won't be a connection in our universes ... and we'd be safe, right?"

"That doesn't solve the problem of the Dark Rose."

Not my issue. Not my universe. "We need to separate our worlds."

"Whatever." Letta pushed past her and strode out of the alley to a street Scarlett didn't recognize. She paused, gaze flickering back and forth, and turned to the right, marching down the road.

"How can you tell he went this way?"

"I just can." With a snort, Letta stuck her nose up. "I know this place better than you do."

Scarlett couldn't argue. The avenue they were on, the shops around them, everything was unfamiliar. They walked in silence until they reached an intersection and both stopped as Scarlett put a hand on Letta's arm. "Where do you think—"

"I don't think. I know where I'm going and where he is. Stop trying to control everything."

"I never realized a copy of me would be such a bitch." Scarlett raised an eyebrow at Letta, who blinked her elaborately penciled eyelids and flicked her middle finger at Scarlett.

"I never realized my copy was so annoying. If you think you can locate the Dark Rose better, why don't you find him yourself?"

"I will. I'll find him before you." Scarlett turned away, trying not to act prissy like Letta, and closed her eyes for a moment. She didn't want to find the Dark Rose—all she wanted to do was fix the intermingling of universes and time loop. In order to repair all that, she probably needed Letta—who disappeared in the opposite direction. If she looked for the Dark Rose, she might find Letta again. Or a way to disconnect their worlds.

If I was evil and wanted to obliterate the world, where would I be?

Scarlett pictured the cloaked guy, standing in the crowded square with his arms spread wide, laughing. She turned in a circle. Around her, high-rise structures rose into the sky.

Who is this Dark Rose? What did we do to him make him angry?

After a moment of hesitation, Scarlett turned down a broad street and started walking. She followed the road, positive she headed towards the center of town.

She paused at the sound of feet padding against the pavement ahead of her and tucked herself behind a garbage can in the shadow of a hat store.

The slapping grew louder, and a figure rounded the corner.

A girl ran toward Scarlett; she looked to be the same age as Scarlett and Letta, with red hair and green eyes slanted like Scarlett's.

Before hesitation stopped her, Scarlett stepped out from behind the trashcan, and the girl jumped back. "Oh, jeez, you scared me. Why aren't you frozen?"

Hair, nose, everything looked the same as Letta, and thus Scarlett. *Oh, jeez. Not another one.* "Uh, I'm not sure." Scarlett shrugged. "Who are you?"

"My name's Carlee. You see anyone else who isn't frozen?"

"One other. Was no one around here before time freaked out?"

Carlee giggled and covered her mouth. "Sorry, no, um, the Dark Rose diverted pretty much everyone in the direction of the square, so most people were either on their way over, or they're already there."

Scarlett bit her lip. "I need to find a way to reverse this time thing. You wanna help?"

"Uh, you mentioned another girl, right? We should find her first. The more assistance we have, the better, right? I mean, I've been wandering around for the past twenty minutes. I even watched someone's head get ripped off by one of those dog-beasts ten times just while I walked. Please don't leave me."

With a wave of her hand, Scarlett turned away. "I'll find a way myself. Good luck finding Letta." She stepped around Carlee and headed down the street by herself again.

"Hey—wait!" Feet slapped against the pavement. Carlee trotted next to her. "Isn't it logical for three people to face this guy rather than two? I mean, he's probably pretty powerful to plan a whole apocalypse by himself."

Scarlett inhaled a breath and exhaled. She closed her eyes, her mind whirring. Three was better than two, but Letta had probably run away. At the same time, two was more helpful than one, and Carlee wanted Scarlett not to leave. At least if she had to face the Dark Rose, she'd have Carlee there, too. She'd keep searching while she helped Carlee find Letta.

"We'll find Letta; she went in that direction."

Carlee's eyes brightened. "I'm sure we can find her."

Twenty minutes later, Scarlett stood with Carlee at the edge of the street on which she and Letta had parted ways.

If I were a prissy teenager looking for a bad guy, where would I be?

That answered nothing, so Scarlett glanced around. "I'm pretty sure she went this way," she said, jogging back toward the spot.

Carlee followed. "There's a beauty salon down here. Do you think she would go in?"

"Of course not." Scarlett sighed and rubbed a hand across her eyes. "She's supposed to be searching for the Dark Rose." *Why would she even ask that?*

Carlee pointed down the road. "The shop is on the corner."

They continued in silence until they reached the corner, and Scarlett peered around. People crowded the street in front of them, all running in different directions. One person stood with their mouth stretched wide in a silent scream.

"This is getting worse." Stepping around a girl writhing on the ground, Scarlett tiptoed through the mess. Why was that avenue scattered with people but Main Street had been clear? Carlee had said the Dark Rose diverted everyone to the square.

"Wait." Carlee grabbed Scarlett's arm. "Over there."

Scarlett squinted in the direction Carlee pointed. Through the horde, but almost indistinguishable, Letta's bright pink cardigan stood out. Scarlett weaved her way towards the other girl.

She fell to her knees next to where Letta writhed on the ground with ropes binding her hands behind her back and a gag covering her mouth.

"Calm down." Scarlett pulled out the gag—a decorative scarf—one she would most certainly wear with some of her outfits back home.

Letta spat, wrinkling her nose. "She needs to learn some fashion sense."

Huh?

"It's black," Letta said as if that explained everything.

With narrowed eyes, Scarlett shook her head. She glanced behind her, but Carlee had disappeared. "Hey, where'd Carlee go?"

"Carlee?"

"Yeah. She looked like us. I think there might be three different universes intermingling right now."

Letta's face paled. "Like us? But—she—I—"

"Take a deep breath."

With a lowered gaze, Letta inhaled and sighed. "Can you untie these for me?" She wiggled her hands behind her back.

"Sure. Who tied you up?"

"Um—well, a *girl* tied me up, and *she* looked like us."

Scarlett's fingers froze on the ropes.

"She had red hair and green eyes," Letta continued, "but I swear she was one of us. Um, and ... it gets worse."

The bindings fell to the ground without a sound as they both stared at each other in silence. Scarlett closed her eyes. "She's working with the Dark Rose, isn't she?"

"Actually, uh ... I think she *is* the Dark Rose."

"I thought he was a guy?"

"Well, we assumed so, but he—sorry, she, always had her hood up."

"How do you know she's, well, *him?*"

"Because I am." Carlee stepped out of the shadows, red hair tumbling down her shoulders. She wore a cloak over her previous outfit, though the hood was lowered and her face was clearly visible. Her hands protruded from the robe, twirling a black rose between three fingers.

"Oh, jeez ..." Scarlett blinked. *Carlee? The Dark Rose? This is even more impossible than everything else so far today.* "Someone wanna explain what's going on?"

"For the love of all that is—" Letta threw her arms into the air and pushed herself to her feet, gesturing at Carlee as she continued, "You're supposed to be smart. I'm the girly girl— the one everyone calls dumb. The one who should probably be blonde. This girl—Carlee, I think you said—is the one who tied me up and left me here and went to find you. I guess she convinced you to come looking for me. She must've wanted us all together. Does everything make sense to you now?"

Scarlett stared. What had gotten into Letta? "Yeah, a little." Scarlett moved her gaze to Carlee.

Carlee tucked the rose behind her ear. The contrast of black on red gave Scarlett the shivers. With a loud crack, Carlee clapped her hands together. "You two helped me quite a bit."

"Helped you how?" Scarlett asked.

"Your connection combined both worlds I wished to destroy, and you've also frozen time long enough for me to set up everything. Now, however, I need it to start again."

"How are you going to do that?"

"Well . . . the two of you touched—which should never have happened. But, because you did, and that's unnatural, the world recognizes that. So, it freezes itself along with the inhabitants, and will keep doing so until the wrong is righted. Which means I just need to eliminate one of you to re-right everything."

She has to kill us. Stumbling to her feet, Scarlett didn't take her gaze off Carlee. With a clearing of her throat, Scarlett held up her hand. "Can I—"

"Shut up." Letta tugged on Scarlett's sleeve. "The faster we get out of here, the better."

She yanked away from Letta. "*Dark Rose,* may I ask you a question before you decide to . . ." *eliminate us* ". . . whatever the plan is?" She didn't wait for Carlee to acknowledge the request before saying, "You're one of us, which means your world is intermingling with ours, as well. So, are you going to destroy your own home, too?"

"Of course not." Carlee flipped her hair over her shoulder in a movement more girly than even what Letta had done. "My world is a distance away. We're a lot more advanced than you, and our technology allows for travel between earths."

"Then, why do you want to destroy ours?" Scarlett asked, a plea in her voice. *Why come all the way to this world to ruin it?*

Carlee fluttered her eyelashes and gave a dreamy sigh. "Because, if only one universe exists, I'll be able to find my soul mate."

All this for a guy? Scarlett snorted. "That's the stupidest logic I've ever heard."

"He must live in it. He's living somewhere, sometimes in more than one location at a time. Like us. And like us—since we share one soul—only one of us can have him. With your worlds gone, I'll be able to find him. For me."

"If he doesn't exist in your world, maybe that's because he's not meant for you."

Carlee's eyes narrowed. "You dare question the Dark Rose?"

Letta tugged on Scarlett's sleeve again. "I think we should leave her be. Let her destroy this world. No big deal. We'll find somewhere else to live."

"She'll kill you along with everything else, Letta." Scarlett shook her head and faced Carlee. "So, you figured you'd waltz into Letta's world, destroy the whole thing and move on to mine?"

Carlee flashed an innocent smile.

"Convenient that our worlds joined—"

"Oh, I brought you two together. At the moment I needed you, you were both concentrating so hard, it was easy enough to interfere with the parts of your mind you weren't using."

"You have psychic powers, too?" Scarlett asked.

"Of course not." Carlee flipped her hair again, rolling her eyes. "We're advanced, I told you already. I merely used technology to interfere with brain waves." She paused and glanced behind her, to where one of the beasts appeared and tore a man's limb off before *poofing* out again. "Unnecessary mess. I should have left the Weres back home. Now, where was I before we got into all this pointless chitchat? Oh, yes, I was telling you how to right the wrong of time freezing so I can get on with my business. Which one of you is first?"

With a squeak, Letta ducked behind Scarlett. "Take her!"

Carlee reached a hand up and pulled a single petal off the flower behind her ear. She held it in her palm and blew. Black dust shimmered around her. Where the powder touched the ground, little holes grew.

One of the pits widened, and Scarlett backed up. She gazed down into the darkness, which looked never ending. "What are those?"

"Portals. To the no-land."

"No-land?"

"The place where a universe exists without a planet. You can step in, or I'll push you. Your choice." Carlee held out the petal and tipped her hand over. The flower fluttered down, its blackness so complete after only a few seconds it was indeterminable from the dark of the portal.

Scarlett watched until it wasn't visible anymore and returned her gaze to the girl in front of her. She bit her lip, glancing sideways and catching Letta in her periphery. Only one of them had to die to separate their planets and return time to normal, but if Scarlett sacrificed herself, Carlee would surely destroy both worlds. Letta was too much of a coward to fight back. Scarlett didn't want to sacrifice an unwilling life to return the order to normal.

If anyone should go, it should be Carlee.

A short distance away, Letta curled into a ball on the ground, rocking back and forth. Her face was red and splotchy from crying. A part of Scarlett wanted to curl up and cry, too.

With a deep breath, Scarlett let out a fierce cry, and threw herself over the smallest portal toward Carlee. Carlee back-pedaled, reaching for the flower in her hair. Scarlett grabbed Carlee's arm, and the rose fluttered down one of the holes. With a scream, Carlee dived after it, but the hole closed over.

Carlee hit Scarlett with such force they both slammed into the dirt, and Scarlett pushed, trying to shift the girl. Carlee's eyes lit up with a manic smile, and she cackled, holding Scarlett down with one hand, chest heaving. Carlee slid something from the inside of her cloak—another rose. Caressing the stem, her face didn't change even as her fingers glided over a thorn and oozed blood. The grin never left, her eyes sparkling with excitement as she pressed her thumb into one of the thorns, making the sharp tip grow.

As the thorn reached the size of a kitchen knife—big enough to stab through a heart—Scarlett didn't think. She kicked her leg up, trying to uproot the other girl.

Carlee remained in place, smiled, and lifted the thorn-knife.

A blur of flesh and flying dark hair hit Carlee in the side, knocking her clean off Scarlett and leaving Letta draped over Scarlett, instead.

As Letta helped her stand, Scarlett released a deep breath. "She almost *murdered* me. I think I'm going to—"

"Don't faint. That's my job." Letta brushed a stray tear off Scarlett's face. "I'm the coward, the one who cries in the corner. You're the brave one. She's the evi—watch out!" Letta shoved Scarlett away as Carlee jumped her. The two rolled across the ground.

Heart pounding in her ears, Scarlett scanned the area. The rose with the thorn-knife had flown from Carlee's hands. Scarlett sprinted over, snatched the thorn up and let out a scream.

Both of the other girls looked up from their struggle.

Carlee patted the hair behind her ear. "No!" she said. "No—"

"What? Is this your last one?" Scarlett smiled, hoping her eyes sparkled in the same manic way as Carlee's had. "Sorry. You'll have to live without." She held the rose out over one of the other portals.

Carlee jerked forward but not in time to stop the rose from disappearing into the darkness.

"No—no, I—" Carlee coughed. She collapsed to her knees, a weird bubbling sound coming up from her mouth. Before Scarlett could wonder what was happening, the Dark Rose disappeared.

A few feet away, Letta stood. "What happened?"

"The rose. She used it before, so I figured it was important. I dropped the second one into a portal, and she, well, disappeared." Scarlett grimaced, and her stomach sank. "Oh, god. I killed her, Letta. I mean, I didn't—"

"Hey …" Letta touched Scarlett's arm. "We both know it had to be done."

"I just need a minute." Scarlett inhaled and let the air out. The tightness in her gut released slightly. "Okay, okay, I think I'll be fine." She buried her face in her hands.

"Remember after we met, you promised to help me find the Dark Rose, if I helped you separate our worlds. You fulfilled your part. Now I'm going to do mine."

Letta stood and jumped toward the black hole, but Scarlet caught her and held on before she could fall in. "I don't need a copy of me to kill themselves for me. I've already killed one myself. I'll be responsible for both." She pulled on Letta, trying to drag her from the hole, but the other girl yanked away.

"Please." Letta closed her eyes. "I did nothing. You found the Dark Rose; you fought her; you killed her. Let me at least do this, so I can be brave, too."

"You're courageous, Letta. You're me." Scarlett smiled. "Bravery might not be your most important trait, but you have it. We share a soul."

A step forward brought Letta to one of the remaining holes. It grew smaller but was still big enough to fit Letta.

"Letta ..." Scarlett joined her other half at the edge of the hole. "We didn't get off to a great start, but—"

"Don't say you'll miss me. Don't say goodbye. I can only be brave for so long before I lose my guts, Scarlett, and if you say goodbye, I don't think I can do this. The holes are closing."

Scarlett swallowed, blinking back tears. Such a short time they'd known each other, yet it seemed like forever. One more step forward, and Letta nodded. Scarlett stifled a squeak as the dark-haired girl tumbled over the ledge.

In a blink, the classroom replaced the broken world. In the far corner, Matthew stared straight ahead of him, his eyes glazed over. Bailey leaned over her desk, probably to copy his work. A few rows in front of her, Jed sat with crossed arms, glasses falling off his nose. Leah fluttered her eyelashes at Toby with a flirty smile.

Whoa. What happened? Scarlett glanced behind her at the clock. *10:30*. Her paper laid in front of her, still frighteningly blank.

"Are you a dummy? Write about yourself."

Scarlett started and whipped around, searching for the owner of the voice. Mr. Krilling, who had been walking down the aisle, stopped at her desk. "Is something wrong, Scarlett?"

She frowned and turned back to face the front. "No, sir. Everything's fine. I thought someone was talking, and I got distracted."

When he moved on, Scarlett snuck another peek behind her. Nobody sat there except Marian, two desks back, her long blonde hair hiding her paper from curious neighbors.

The whole thing you just thought you saw was in your mind.

"We're right here."

"Actually," another voice said, "We've always been here. You needed to meet us before you could realize."

Letta? Carlee? Scarlett dropped her head into her hands. *You've got to be kidding. Now my dreams are following me even when I'm awake?*

"We're not dreams. We're you. Now you know."

Scarlett stifled a shiver and set her pencil to the paper. Voices in her head. Her own thoughts—all from a daydream.

"Not a dream."

"Not a dream."

How did I meet you, if you're not a hallucination? Scarlett bit her lip. *Arguing with myself. Is that normal?*

"Look at your hair, you idiot."

My hair? Scarlett pulled a strand in front of her eyes and stifled a gasp. Her hair was black. *Like ... Letta's.*

How come nobody else noticed?

"To them, this is you. You never saw yourself until now."

Scarlett clutched her pencil tighter. So had it all happened? Had the world almost ended?

I almost died ...

And I killed Carlee.

"You didn't. I'm right here. Now you need to finish this exam. Only twenty-five minutes left."

I have nothing to write about, though.

A squeaking sort of sound, almost like laughter invaded her thoughts.

"Write about us. Write about you. Write about what life means now that you understand what a true sacrifice is."

Scarlett set her pen to the paper. *Often in life, we do not real-*

ize that our greatest sacrifices come not just from our hearts, but the different parts of our souls ...

Acknowledgements

To Mom and Dad—thanks for putting up with me through my writing phases, even when all I ever wanted to do was sit at the computer. You taught me how to balance my writing and my life. But who needs balance, anyway, right? Love you guys!

Marissa Halvorson

Marissa's dream of writing came about when she was ten, after reading a particularly inspiring story of dragons and elves. She instantly fell in love with the fantasy genre, and characters soon began to manifest to satisfy her adoration. It started with a forty page handwritten novel, which she dubbed "Dragon Girl" and continued on to more challenging (and better written) works.

Now, Marissa can often be found to be studying literature in English class, curled up at home with one book or another, or with her eyes glued to the computer screen as her newest set of characters manifest.

Dragon Flight

J. Keller Ford

J. Taylor Publishing

I grip the handles of the harness and squeeze my eyes tight as the coaster tops the three-hundred foot lift.

Oh, geez. What was I thinking? I hate heights. I hate things that go fast. Not a great combo for rollercoaster riding.

My pulse thumps in my throat as the metal beast curves to the left. I squeeze my eyes so tight they hurt. *Oh, no. Here we go. Here we go.* The scream hangs in my throat, waiting for the drop.

It doesn't come. The steel dragon jerks to a halt, with me in the front row and nowhere to look but out and down.

What? No, no, no. We're not supposed to stop! I've watched this ride a gazillion times. It never stops. I picture the track in my mind. Up, around, down, flip, corkscrew, insanity, heart attack. One and a half minutes of terrifying scream time. *No. This can't be happening! Why? Why now? Why did I get on this ride?*

The answer sits in the seat next to me. Dean McCall. Damn his tall, dark-haired good looks and jewel-blue eyes. I've crushed on him since sophomore year, ever since he showed up in Mr. Wilkins' history class wearing a pair of oh-my-God-nice-butt jeans and a Halo game T-shirt. I tried then not to salivate like Pavlov's dog, but it was useless. Not much has changed since, as I'm pretty sure I just about melted out of my skin when he cornered me by the popcorn stand and asked if I wanted to ride Dragon Flight with him.

Me! Book nerd extraordinaire.

So what if he waited for Grad night to notice me ? No one's perfect, right? I gulped, mesmerized by his hypnotic eyes and charming, spearmint smile, and uttered something intelligent like, "Uh-huh." Of course, my insides turned all gooey, and my heart struck up a crazy fast Congo beat because I'm such a feet-on-the-ground kind of gal. My brain shouted, *Speak, you dolt! Tell him no. Tell him you're afraid of heights. He'll understand.* Instead, I shook my head and said, "I-I ... okay."

Major face palm, but really, I had no choice. It was Dean McCall, and if I turned him down, I'd look like a moron in front of everyone who was anyone. Besides, who better to face my fears with than the cutest guy to ever walk the halls of Newbury High? Now, as I sit stranded at the top of this freaking ride, I'm beginning to question that logic.

I press my head back against the coaster's seat. *Get a grip, Amber. Breathe deep. You're okay. You're strapped in. You're not going anywhere.*

Clunk. Clunk.

My eyes spring open.

What was that?

I fight back the urge to scream.

The harness releases and lifts off my shoulders, its movement stopped by the belt latched to the seat. I squeak like a frightened mouse and clutch the restraint tight to my chest, my knuckles as white as the moon staring down at me. *Oh, God, I'm gonna die.*

A cool breeze brushes across my face. Lightning zigzags across the sky. *Oh, no, please don't rain. Please.* Tears pool in the corners of my eyes. My chest aches from too many shallow breaths. *Stop it, Amber! Get a grip! You don't hear anyone else getting upset, do you?*

I listen for nervous laughter, screams, talking, any sort of hysterical chatter, but I hear nothing. Not a word. Not a laugh. A fist knots in my stomach. I swallow and force a single word from my parched mouth. "Dean?"

Silence.

My stomach flips upside down and inside out.

"Umm, hello? Dean?"

His name hangs in the air like thick smoke on a stagnant hot summer night. I lean forward and tilt my head to the right.

A smidgeon of a scream escapes in a whisper. The remaining fragment sticks in my throat, choking my airway. Dean sits frozen in his seat, a wide grin glued to his face, his arms extended above his head. The guy next to him and the girl on the end are stuck in the same position. Human statues petrified in time.

What the freak?

"Dean? Talk to me. Please." I wipe my sweaty palms on my jeans.

Nothing.

A chill settles inside me. I force myself to stay calm. "Dean?" I raise my voice. "Hel-lo? Anyone?"

The park is silent. No music from the park's speakers or the arcades. *Am I deaf?* The rhythmic tapping of my fingers on the harness prove I'm not.

More lightning sizzles across the sky. I tense when the lights on the track flicker a few times and go out. The rest of the lights in the park follow. Blip. Blip. I'm in complete darkness.

What the heck?

I take several deep breaths and count to ten. It's an old trick I learned a long time ago to slow my breathing and clear the dizziness when it begins to swarm like moths on a streetlamp.

I focus on the track of the steel beast, rising and falling, twisting and coiling, determined to carry me to the depths of its lair. I can't let it. I have to get down. I have to find out what is wrong and why everyone is frozen in time like victims of some modern day Pompeii disaster.

I shake off a chill as an imaginary headline flashes before my eyes: *Acrophobic falls to her death while climbing from faulty thrill ride.* I banish the thought from my head. I have no intentions of dying. Not that way. Still, my brain fails to fire on all synapses, refuses to come up with any ideas on how to complete my insane, idiotic act of heroism, until I fix my gaze on the narrow metal path to freedom.

Steps! Of course! How else do thrill-seeking maintenance workers fix these damn things when they break down? It seems simple enough—get out of my seat, walk a short distance along the catwalk to the steps and take them to the ground. Easy peasy.

Not!

The mere thought of it sends my body into lockdown mode, which is where I remain for quite some time, until I get the insatiable urge to pee. *Why didn't I go before I got on the ride?* I can no longer delay the inevitable. I reach between my legs and release the belt from the seat.

The harness lifts over my head with a whoosh.

The lack of restraints suck the breath out of my lungs like a vacuum hose on a garment bag. I dig my nails into my thighs. *Oh, God, I can't do this! I'm going to die! I'm going to die.*

Anger kicks in. *No you're not! Now pull yourself together! You know what you have to do. Do it!*

I start humming some old tune my mom used to sing when my dad left, something about surviving. I lift off my butt, hold tight to the seatbelt, and ease to the floor. I sit stock-still, knees to my chest, my body shaking like the San Andreas Fault in a nine-point-o earthquake. I glance over at Dean, still not moving, oblivious to my insane act of stupidity. I snort. *It's just as well.*

I shake out my arms and steady my breathing. *One. Two. Three.* Butterflies take flight in my stomach. I get on my hands and knees and pray. *You can do this, Amber. Come on.* I crawl toward the opening.

Oh, crap.

I rock back and forth; my palms teeter on the edge of the coaster. The ground. It's so far down. One wrong move and I will fall! *Go! Crawl out! The catwalk is right there!*

My bottom lip trembles. A few stray tears fall through the rails of the track. "I can't," I sob. My limbs wobble.

You have to!

I wipe my tears on my sleeve, hold my breath, and take a gigantic step forward. My breath hitches for a moment before I tumble onto the cold, steel bars of the track.

As if touched with a hot poker, I scramble across a narrow metal beam to the catwalk, my heart thudding in my ears. I lay on my stomach, tremors rattling my legs. Closing my eyes, I'm anxious to rid my body of the overwhelming urge to scream. How helpless, numb and terrified I am. I stare at the shadowed ground below me, desperate for its solidness beneath my feet. *The steps. Back up.*

I army-crawl backward on my stomach, my side pressed against the low metal wall encasing the steps. Elation ripples through me as my feet find the first rung. *You did it, Amber Jenkins! Back up! Don't stop! Don't look down! Go!*

The steps rattle beneath my weight as I shimmy down. I daydream of summer nights on the lake. Baking cupcakes. Imagining what it would be like to kiss Dean.

My foot slips. I slide downward at NASCAR speed, reaching for the rungs, but they elude my grasp. My ribs scream in agony with each crashing thud against the metal. My chin smacks the steps, and I bite my tongue; blood trickles down my throat.

Like tires over a never-ending railroad track, I slide off the bottom step onto the pavement and fold in a heap. My head throbs as if cleaved in two, and I roll onto my back and wipe the tears from my eyes. Above me, the belly of the coaster comes into view. I laugh. I can't help it. I made it. Maybe not gracefully, but I made it.

Rolling onto my hands and knees, I stand. My bladder pulses with the reminder of how much I need to pee. A restroom waits between a souvenir shop and a funnel cake stand—both silent. Inky darkness falls over me like a weightless sheet as I limp inside, and with my arms held out zombie style, I shuffle forward.

"Come on, stalls, where are you?"

My hands hit something solid. Warm.

"What the heck?"

I pat the object, touching, feeling. Fabric. Hair. Eyes. Nose. I gasp and clamp my hand over my mouth. Backing up, I bump into another something-or-other behind me. Another brushes my leg. Pee trickles down my leg and puddles on the floor.

Rushing out the way I came in, I'm chilled as if possessed by a ghost. I shudder and cry as sweat pours from my brow and along the nape of my neck. *What was that? People frozen in there in the dark? I touched them! Ewww!* The heebee-jeebies crawl all over me.

Running inside the gift shop, I rifle through the racks and pick out a towel, a pair of shorts, a T-shirt and some flip-flops. I tear off the tags and leave them, along with a fifty, on the counter next to the cash register. Hurrying back to the bathroom, I feel my way along the wall. A sigh of relief escapes as I reach a sink and find it unoccupied. Public bathroom soap never smelled so good.

Stepping into a patch of moonlight, I unfold a map I clipped from a guy standing outside a coffee shop. As suspected, the security and park offices are located at the front—completely opposite of where I am.

I head to my right, down the main walkway, past fleshy statues of lovers kissing, babies crying in strollers and birds stuck in flight. I stop for a moment, to pet an owl perched on a wood railing, when a strange darkness envelops the sky and obliterates the moon and stars.

What the ... I close my eyes and breathe deep, certain I'm mistaken, but when I open my eyes, the veil remains. *First petrified people, now disappearing celestial bodies?* Shivering, I tuck my hair behind my ear and keep walking. I have to get help.

A water ride appears on my left. The log carrying seven people is frozen in motion at the bottom of the hill with the splashdown arced in a frozen spray over their heads. Faces smile, shoulders hunch in anticipation of a grand soaking. The scene is surreal, as if I stepped into a photograph and can't get out.

My stomach lurches with dread. What if the entire world, the universe, is stuck for all eternity in suspended animation?

Why aren't I?

A breeze rolls over me. It rustles my hair and plays with the banner over the ride's entrance. A glimmer of hope flickers inside. Something moved other than me. Granted, it's slight, but slight is better than nothing.

I hurry on, passing one food stand after another, people

sitting at tables, their hotdogs and hamburgers on the way to their mouths but unreached. My stomach grumbles, and I snatch a slice of pizza and a drink from a woman with so many diamonds on her hands, she could buy Miami with a single bauble. I figure, what the hell. Maybe I can pay her back sometime. When the world is set right again. If ever.

Devouring the food, I trudge up the landscaped hill. The kiddy ride section is on my right, the Leviathan coaster to my left. Two trains are stuck on it—one going up, one stuck in mid-loop. My entire body cringes. *Those poor people!* I want to cry for them. It doesn't make sense why everything stopped. It makes less sense why I'm the only one who is unaffected.

Maybe I'm dreaming? What if I'm not? What if I can't find anyone to help me? What if the security people are frozen, too? Where are the main controls to the rides and the lights? My head hurts from all the chatter inside of it. *Baby steps, Amber. Baby steps.*

I stop at the bottom of the hill beside the Ferris wheel and unfold my map. I need to turn right, go past the carousel and turn left. I'm almost there.

A *chk chk* noise makes the hair on my arms stand on end. I spin around. Something big is coming toward me, and it's nothing I recognize. My stomach lurches. The sound grows louder, nearer. I duck behind a trashcan, unsure of the thing-amajig marching my way.

Chk. Chk. Chk.

I peek around the corner, ready to shout for help, but the words are lost by my own scream, as four Rottweiler-sized cockroaches scurry into view, their mandibles clicking away.

This can't be real. I'm dreaming. I have to be dreaming!

They turn their heads to the right and left before taking off, two in my direction.

I get up and run.

Chk. Chk. Chk.

An antenna brushes my leg. I scream and spurt into over-drive, past a line of gift shops. I hook a right at the fork in the path, and crash into a throng of human statues standing every-where. I mean everywhere. Hundreds of them, frozen, mouths open as if laughing. I push my way through, bouncing off them like a metal ball in a pinball game. A few of them fall over, but I don't care. All I can do is run, the cool air seizing my throat.

I glance behind me, praying I've outrun the bugs. They are nowhere to be seen. I stumble forward, gasping for breath. A very tall man stares down at me, poised like a department store mannequin waiting for his turn in a window display. I wipe my tears as hysteria takes over, and laugh and cry at the same time. I can't help it. My life is freaky in the most macabre, twisted sort of way.

"I have got to be dreaming!"

The carousel comes into view on my left, the colorful metal horses stretched in full gallop as if trying to run from their fate. I long to break the spell on them, reanimate them so they can rise and fall to the calliope music.

I pass the turnstiles at the entrance of the park and hurry toward the sky-ride and the park offices. Shadows of buildings loom behind a fence marked *Employee Entrance. Authorized Admittance Only.*

After what I just experienced, I dare anyone to tell me I'm not authorized, not that anyone would because I'm the only one not frozen.

I push open the gate and pass a line of electric carts and immobile employees shoving trash carts. I wonder how much time has passed since everything froze. Is it the whole world or just here? Picturing Dean, his gorgeous smile, the way his hair sweeps over one eye. I hear the soft melody of his voice in my head and worry I'll never see him again. I have to get Granbury Park up and running again.

Behind the scenes is much bigger than I ever imagined. There are entire buildings dedicated to costumes, props, musical instruments and set designs, but I'll be darned if I can find the administrative buildings.

I turn down an alley and almost run into two performers on stilts; they're dressed in feathered costumes, their faces painted like peacocks. Up ahead is a tree-lined path marked *Employee Exit.* Shadows of buildings loom in the distance.

My destination lies at the end of the road. It has to. A breeze wafts over me, carrying with it the scent of night-blooming jasmine. I breathe it in, swimming in its intoxicating sweetness, and continue walking, drawing nearer to the buildings. I tilt my head back and take in the flowering archway of wisteria above me. Beyond it, I hear the most wonderful sound in the world—a voice. A muffled male voice.

My heart leaps. I sprint forward.

"Hello?" My voice is so loud it cracks the silence. "Can you hear me? Hello?"

A deafening commotion rattles overhead. I emerge from the archway and freeze as a dome lifts from the park, exposing what appears to be striped curtains, a desk lamp ... and a bunk bed? Rubbing my eyes does nothing; the scenery remains the same.

I amble ahead, keeping to the shadows of the alleyway. My heart is pounding, my brain flipping out. The only logical explanation for what I see doesn't compute. It's impossible to have worlds within worlds.

"Come on, work this time. Please?" The male speaks again, this time his voice louder, clearer.

The tapping of fingers on what sounds like a keyboard fills

the air. *What the freak?* A high-pitch tone follows a few loud sequential beeps.

My hands fly to my ears. "Stop it! Turn it off!" The pain is excruciating.

"What? Huh?" The guy's voice is so loud.

The tone stops and is replaced by another sound that can only be described as a chair scraping across the floor. A face pops over the edge of my universe.

I'm not sure who screams the loudest, me or the blond-haired, brown-eyed boy staring down at me, mouth open.

"What? Huh? How?" he says, echoing my own thoughts.

I cower against the side of a building, every inch of my body trembling. My mouth tries to move, but all I can do is stare and shake like a plucked guitar string.

"W-who are you?" the boy asks, never taking his gaze off me. His face is pale, and I'm pretty sure I'm the last thing he expected to see.

Once I find my voice, I counter him in a battle of wits. "Y-you first. Where am I?"

"Holy crap!" His warm breath falls on me, covering me in a fog of peanut butter and jelly. He disappears for a moment and returns, moving as if he's sitting on a roll-around chair. "This is freaking awesome! You're real. You're actually real." He smiles and claps his hands. His enthusiasm isn't contagious.

I venture out of the shadows, and glare at him, my arms folded across my chest. "Of course I'm real, moron. What else would I be?"

"No, no. That's just it. You can't be real. It's an impossibility, but here you are." His grin widens. "This is like the most amazing thing that has ever happened to me." He leans forward, his ginormous face in clear view above me. If there could ever be a man in the moon, it would be him. "Hi," he says, flashing a mouth full of braces. "My name is Josh. Josh Granbury. Welcome to my theme park creation, Granbury Park."

Confusion rushes over me like a tidal wave. *His creation? What's he talking about?* Granbury Park isn't his creation. It's been here for decades and he can't be more than eighteen. I pinch myself to prove I'm not in a dream, but I must be. It's the only thing that makes sense.

Humor him. If I do, maybe this dream guy will tell me how to fix whatever is wrong, so I can get Dean and the others off that rollercoaster and get out of here. I smile up at him and say, "Nice to meet you, Josh. I'm Amber. Amber Jenkins."

"Hmm, Amber Jenkins." He taps his finger to his lip and rolls out of view. He comes back a moment later, a black and white composition book in his hand. He flips through the pages, and stops. "Here you are. Amber Irene Jenkins, acrophobic, oldest of three kids. Parents divorced. Likes water skiing and baking cupcakes. Prefers hammocks to real beds."

I stare at him, mouth open. "H-how do you know that stuff about me?"

"I know everything about everyone in Granbury Park. I should, since I created all of you. It's all right here." He waves the comp book in the air.

"Yeah, right." So dream guy thinks he's the Creator? *Just go with it, Amber. You have to find out if he can help you.* "So, um, what's wrong with everything in Granbury Park? Why is everything frozen?" I dare not mention the human-size roaches. He'll think I'm nuts.

He tosses his book to the side and combs his fingers through his hair. "I don't know. I've run the program a million times. I've checked the wiring, the connections. Everything is where it's supposed to be. It sucks, because if I don't find the solution tonight, I'm in deep crap."

"I'm sorry. I'm confused." Funny thing is, I really am.

Josh stands, and I draw in a deep breath. I have entered a dreamland of giants. "Granbury Park is the final project for my computer programming class. I've been working on it all year long, building all the rides, laying all the electrical wires so they'll run. I made all the buildings, bought and installed all the plants. I can't tell you how many hours I spent coming up with all the characters, you included, and incorporating that program into the one that runs the park."

"Wait, wait. Are you telling me I'm a computer program?"

"Yeah, and a pretty darn good one, too. Somehow, I made you real but only in a virtual sense. I can see you, talk to you, you can interact with me. In short, you're a learner, but I'm pretty sure if you tried to leave the park, you'd glitch."

I give him a stern look. "I'd glitch. Riiiiight."

"No, I'm serious. Try. Go on. Leave." His gigantic finger, wound in a band aid, points to a door marked *Exit*.

I take his challenge and head for the door. It's time to show Mr. Josh Granbury I can go anywhere I want without issue.

I push the door open. With a confident smirk on my face, I take a step over the threshold.

My leg turns into snowy static, much like tuning into a television channel that is off the air. I stumble back and kick the door closed with my foot.

"O.M.G.! This can't be happening. Wake up!" I stagger around, my palms pressed to my temples. "Come on, Amber, wake up." I pinch myself a few times, just to make sure I get the message. Red welts stand high on my arms, the sting throbbing from each one of them.

Josh chuckles. "Do you like inflicting pain upon yourself? Interesting."

"Shut up, and go away," I say, "unless you can wake me up

from this nightmare!"

"Yeah, well, that's kind of hard to do when you're not asleep."

His pursed lips and told-you-so eyes tell me everything I need to know, and it's not what I want to hear. My heart sinks in my stomach as I fight back the tears. "I don't believe you," I say, my voice a trembling mess. "I can't be a computer program. I just can't."

Josh sits in his chair and stares down at me with big puppy dog eyes. "Answer me this: where were you born?"

I search my brain. It comes up blank.

"When's your birthday?"

Again, another blank.

"What are you parents' names? How old is your brother? What happened at school today?"

I shake my head. "I don't know! I can't remember!" More of his questions fly my way. "Stop it! Why are you doing this to me?"

His voice softens. "I have to make you see you're not real, Amber. You're a figment of my imagination. Everything you remember, I programmed into you. You and Dean? It's all a program. A video game, except, instead of playing it on the computer, I designed it to play on a real set. But something's wrong, and I can't figure it out. All I know is, if I don't fix it, and it's not ready to present to my class in less than seven hours, I'm going to fail my computer class. If I fail my class, I lose my chance at a scholarship. Lose my scholarship, I don't go to college. I don't go to college, I become a plumber like my dad, not that being a plumber is bad. Some folks, like my dad, make great plumbers. But I want more. If I have to resort to plumbing, my life will be over. My world will end. I'll be finished. I'll end up flushing crap out of people's drains for the rest of my life, instead of designing and programming the next big thing in virtual gaming systems. I have to make this work."

Poor kid. I take a moment to ponder what he said. He has more pending on getting these rides going than I do. I try to remember if I ever had a goal of going to college. I can't even think it. So much of my life is empty, because I don't have one. Literally.

I sit on a bench and consider my options. Even though our reasons are different, Josh and I want the same thing—to get Granbury Park operational again. I stand and face him.

"I'll help you under one condition. Since I have no life to speak of, I'd like, for one exceptional moment, to pretend I do. You have to program Dean to kiss me when he gets off the ride. In front of everyone. And he has to ask me to prom. Oh, and one more thing—you need to program out all my scrapes and bumps and bruises I got when I scrambled from Dragon Flight."

Josh shakes his head. "I can't do that ... you know ... take away the bruises and stuff. That's not part of the program. You did that on your own."

"But you said I'm not real. How can I get bruises and cuts if I'm not real?"

"I told you, I don't know. It might be a glitch in the program. I didn't design any of my characters to function on their own. I think when the park shut down, a runtime error occurred, somehow allowing your individual program to alter. It sounds irrational to me, but it's all I've got. Unfortunately, it means you'll have to face Dean McCall with a whole new look. If you're okay with that, I can make everything else you want to happen, happen."

I take a moment to consider his idea. Sure, I'd like to not be all banged up when I get my first real kiss, but what the heck? Maybe seeing my battle wounds will make Dean want me even more.

I smile. "You've got yourself a deal, Josh Granbury. What do you need from me?"

Hours pass and Josh grows more frustrated. Nothing we come up with is working, and plumbing is beginning to look like his only viable option for a future occupation.

"Damn it!" he says, banging his head on the table. "How hard can it be to locate a freaking bug?"

My ears perk up as I yawn. "Bugs? You're searching for bugs?"

He looks at me, bags under his tired, bloodshot eyes. "Yeah. That's what we call the glitches that infect a computer program."

"Well, why didn't you say so, earlier, dingbat? I saw four of them crawling around the Ferris wheel. Nasty, gross suckers."

Josh's face lit up. "The Ferris wheel? Are you sure?"

I nod.

His face breaks open in a wide grin. "Amber Jenkins, if I could kiss you, I would!"

He rolls across the room out of my sight. I hear finger-tapping and words like *Eureka* and *Yeah, baby* energizing the room.

Before long, lampposts in Granbury Park switch on. Carousel music fills the air. Arcade games fire up.

I laugh and run down the alleyway, back to the entrance of the park. "Josh, you did it!" I clap my hands and jump up and down. "This is amazing. How did you—"

He hovers over the park. "It was easy once you told me where to look. I wrote the program so well, the code sort of gelled. It looked so *right*. The problem was so subtle, a transposition of letters, I doubt Bill Gates would have found it."

"Who's Bill Gates?"

Josh laughs. "It doesn't matter. Are you ready to get back on your ride?"

"So soon?"

"Sorry. I have to get to school, which means shutting this all down, loading it in the truck and getting there before seven-thirty."

"Can you put me on the ride as the coaster pulls into the station?" I bat my eyes and try to look all five-year old cute.

"And have Dean flip out because you're not sitting next to him? The poor guy will assume you fell out, and he'll have a heart attack."

"But I'll have a heart attack if I ride the thing."

Josh laughs again. "No, you won't. I promise. You're in very capable, programming hands." He wiggles his fingers.

I love his smile. It's comforting.

"I promise you'll survive, and just imagine the payout when the ride is over." Josh smiles and winks.

Blood rushes to my cheeks. I hope he doesn't notice, not that it matters. After all, I'm only a computer program, a character in a game. I can't die. I can't have a heart attack, but I can have the most wonderful ending to my evening. A smile slides across my face. "Okay. You win, but you have to promise to tell me if you pass your class. I won't be truly happy until I know you're not going to flush crap for a future. I have to know you're going to follow your dreams, and get what you want, too."

"You got it. Ready?"

I look into his face, his eyes brighter than I've ever seen. "Yeah, I'm ready."

He disappears from sight, and the taps begin again. Seconds later, I'm aboard Dragon Flight, the harness over my shoulders, the belt latched to the seat.

Josh appears above me, holding my sky—a plastic dome—off to the side. "Are you okay?" he asks.

I glance over at Dean, still frozen in time, and smile. "Yeah, I'm good." I turn back to my rescuer. "Josh? In case I never see you again ... thanks, for everything."

"You're welcome." His voice falters. "I-I'm sorry you can't be real."

I shake my head. "It's okay. No regrets. No apologies, okay? It's all good. Now get to school so I can get down from this ride."

His soft, milk chocolaty eyes melt my heart. "Thanks, Amber. I'll never forget you." The color of night falls over me again like a protective shield.

I grip the handles of the harness and squeeze my eyes tight as the coaster tops the three-hundred foot lift.

My pulse thumps in my throat as the metal beast curves to the left. I squeeze my eyes so tight they hurt. *Oh, no. Here we go. Here we go.*

My stomach lurches. Wind rushes past me as the steel dragon plunges toward the ground. Up we go, flipping over in a corkscrew.

I scream and laugh at the same time as the monstrosity rips and roars over the track. Never in my life have I felt so exhilarated and free.

The ride reaches the end and glides into the station. At the stop of the cars, our harnesses release. Dean lifts me from my seat and we run down to the exit, my hand in his.

"Oh, my gosh! That was amazing!" He takes me in his arms and spins me around, my legs swinging outward. His hair's a mess, his eyes glistening as bright as the moon and stars above, and he's grinning more than I've ever seen before. "Ride with me again!" he says, setting me on the ground.

"I-I don't know."

He faces me, his eyes full of concern and worry, and brushes my hair away from my face. He caresses the bump on my chin. "How did you get hurt? What happened to you?"

I'm touched by his sincerity. "I don't know. I must have hit it on the harness, or something."

His gaze sweeps over me, brow drawn in confusion. A slew of questions must be lining up behind his eyes, but like a good computer program, he smiles and says, "You know, Amber. This might seem sudden, but I've been wondering ... would you like to go to prom with me?"

Schoolgirl giddiness erupts inside, but I force myself to stay calm and cool on the outside. I drape my arms around his neck, and say, "I thought you'd never ask."

His cheeks pink up, and he engulfs me in a giant hug. Inside, my heart swells with happiness, so much I'm sure I'll explode. Behind him, a message streams across a digital marquee: *I passed! I'm going to college! I owe you the world, Amber Jenkins!*

I smile. A tear of joy escapes down my cheek.

Dean lifts my chin, his breath hovering at my lips. "Are you okay?" He brushes his thumb across my cheek.

A message flashes across the marquee—*It's time.*

I nod and smile. A tear falls.

"Are you sure," Dean asks.

"Positive." I run my fingers through his hair and smile. "Kiss me."

His lips, soft and warm, press against mine. My foot pops behind me.

The marquee overhead flashes another message.

Ready for more programming?

My belly tingles, and I can't help but giggle. *Oh, yeah, baby.
Am I ever.*

I drift into temporary oblivion, wrapped in the arms of the
cutest guy ever to walk the halls of Newbury High. I have no
idea what tomorrow will bring, but I can't wait to see what the
brilliant mind of Josh Granbury comes up with next.

Acknowledgements

There are so many to thank it is difficult to know where to begin.

To God, my Lord and Savior, thank you for the gift you have given me. I promise to not squander it.

To my husband and kids, thank you for putting up with me and understanding my need for personal space and writing time. To my son, Kevin, a special thank you for your eyes and blatant teen honesty.

To Jennifer Eaton, Julie Reece and all my other writing sisters at The Sisterhood of the Traveling Pens…I would be lost without your friendship and unwavering support. My life and writing is richer because of each of you. To Jamie and Diane: Ft. Myers holds a special place in my heart because of you. Thank you for everything.

Finally, to my fellow bloggers, blog followers, book reviewers, friends, extended family — thank you from the bottom of my heart for believing in me and tagging along on my journey. I cannot express in words how much you are appreciated.

J. Keller Ford

J. Keller Ford is a quirky mother of four, grand-mother and scribbler of young adult fantasy tales. She has an insatiable appetite for magic, dragons, knights and faeries, and weaves at least one into every story she conceives. Her muse is a cranky old meadow gnome that follows her everywhere she goes and talks incessantly, feeding her ideas for stories 24/7.

When she's not writing or blogging, the former Corporate Paralegal enjoys listening to smooth jazz, collecting seashells, swimming, bowling, riding roller coasters and reading. Jenny lives minutes from the beaches of the west coast of Florida with her husband of twenty years, her two sons and a pair of wacky cats and three silly dogs. The pets have trained her well.

The 13th Month

L.S. Murphy

J. Taylor Publishing

December 31st, 2013, 4:01pm

"Stop being a douche, Jackie. This end of the world crap is nothing but a load of ... well, crap. Get over it." I snatched our shared laptop from my little brother and closed the lid, not bothering to check out the site he'd become fixated on during the last hour. Jackie's conspiracy theories were a constant pain in my ass.

"Give it back, Nixon." He whined, reaching across my body as I shoved the ancient computer behind my back. "This one's real. I'm telling you; it's gonna to happen."

"Just like you said Rapture was real, right? Or the Mayan prophecy of December twenty-first in two-thousand twelve?" I shoved his thirteen-year-old body away from me. "Guess what, dipshit? Twenty-twelve has come and gone with the world still spinning. Get outta here so I can chat with my girl."

Jackie stood, brushing invisible dirt off his green plaid shorts. In a few years, he'd either be modeling or coming out of the closet. I swore my brother got all the looks in the family—Mom's California blonde hair, Dad's bright blue eyes, and at least two inches taller than I was.

Me? I inherited Dad's brown hair that curled if it got too long and Mom's brown eyes the color of dry dirt. In other words, boring.

"One of these days, you'll believe me," Jackie said, his voice deeper than normal. His eyes sparkled like ice held up to a light bulb. "The end is coming. Everything will stop. And there's nothing you can do to prevent it."

"Dude, did you forget your Zoloft, or something? What's with the voice?" I fell onto my twin bed, wishing for the millionth time I had my own room. The computer lay across my thighs, warming the denim beneath it.

Flipping me the bird, Jackie left the room and slammed our door behind him, rattling the windows from the force. The little shit must've started lifting weights. I glanced over to his half of the room but saw no sign that my brother had suddenly decided to add to his martial arts workout. Instead, his side was spotless, with a perfectly made bed, organized desk, laid-out clothes, and his lined-up tae kwon do ribbons. Jackie switched disciplines when he was seven, while I stuck with karate. I would've quit, but girls thought it was sexy. Laura included.

My shit was less than perfect. A box shoved into the closet hid my wrinkled karate ribbons. Homework and textbooks littered my desk. Even our matching blue plaid comforters were opposites—mine faded and wrinkled, his smooth and bright like the day Mom bought it.

Shaking my head, I opened the laptop and typed in the password. Laura was far more important than worrying about what was up little bro's butt. Especially since we had big plans that night. Her parents would be out ringing in twenty-fourteen at some hotel soiree, leaving the house to us. Alone. Six years of crushing on her and six months of dating her were leading to what I hoped would be the best night of my life.

The computer's fan struggled to whirr as the screen woke. The website Jackie'd been jacking off to popped up. I glanced at the clock in the lower right-hand corner. My video chat with Laura wouldn't start for a few minutes, so I had time to see what my bro was checking out. Why couldn't he be into porn, like most guys?

I almost laughed at the ticking clock on the front page. Every end of the world website had one. They seemed kind of pointless. If the world was going to end, a warning wouldn't be splayed out on a website.

Two opposing angels stared at one another from the upper corners. Their arms extended over the top of the screen, pointing with fingers touching. The graphic was pretty cool, better than most I'd seen, until the angel on the right turned and smiled. Then it was the *best* graphic I'd ever seen.

I waited for the other angel to do the same, but he didn't. Instead, the clock flashed at me. Eight hours until the end of the world. The angels and the clock faded into the background as white cursive text appeared as if someone was writing on the monitor.

Dude who built the site did an amazing job. I still had two minutes before I needed to video Laura, so I started reading.

At the end of the thirteenth year, death and mercy will meet during the thirteenth month to determine the course of humanity. Time will stop. Life will cease until one dies.

The words faded into the background as another line faded in.

If death wins, life continues.

Faded.

If mercy wins, life changes. appeared.

If neither defeats the other before the end of the thirteenth day of the thirteenth month of the thirteenth year, life ends.

The last two words pulsed like nightclub strobe lights before merging into the homepage with the clock and angels. If I believed in that bullshit, the world would end in less than eight hours. I stared at the angel who had turned its head. As if by my own will, it did it again, but it wasn't smiling.

'You', it mouthed.

I jerked back in my bed. *No way that just happened. No freaking way.* My heart pounded against my ribs. The angel continued to stare at me. His gaze intensified, holding my own. Fire blazed in his pupils. Flames danced and swayed, my body moving to their rhythm.

The blips of the video chat calling yanked me back to reality. I opened the icon and hit answer.

"Nix, there you are," Laura said. The scowl turning her pretty lips into a frown was enough to know I'd screwed up.

"Sorry, Jackson had the computer. He's like a leech with this stupid thing." I glanced at the clock, realizing I was more than ten minutes behind schedule. *Stupid freaking website.*

Since the moment Laura Flaggart moved to Taos, when we were eleven, I'd been in love with her. Her strawberry blonde hair, the freckles splattered over her nose, and her knowing hazel eyes, hooked me the first time she punched me in the arm. Freshman year, she started dating Jason Parker. Sophomore year, she dated Harry Lay. Junior year, she went out with Michael Fitzpatrick, Gordon Nin, and Frank Grant. Each time she was single, I'd ask her out. She'd always said no.

Until six months ago.

"He found another conspiracy to get hooked on," I said.

"Really?" Laura's eyes lit up. She enjoyed conspiracy theories almost as much as Jackie, but for different reasons. "What is it?" She'd gotten to know my little bro well since she agreed to go out with me. He practiced flirting with her. It drove me crazy, because Laura flirted back.

"The Thirteenth Month. Ever heard of it?" I still had the site open on the left side of the screen. The angel no longer stared at me. I wasn't sure if I should be disappointed, or not.

"No, I haven't. What site was he looking at?" She typed it as I rattled it off to her. Laura's eyebrows creased, and her forehead wrinkled. "Give it to me again." The expression never left her face as her eyes pointed off toward the left. Her fingers bounced against the springy keyboard. Laura typed like she played the piano, her long fingers leaping off the keys and almost smacking herself in the face. "Are you sure you're reading that right? It won't come up here."

I copied the URL into an email and sent it to her even though I knew I'd given it to her correctly. "Check your email."

"Keeps saying the site doesn't exist." She sat back in her chair, arms crossed over her chest. That was a sad thing. Her chest should never be covered. "That's just weird. I wonder if Jackson made it up, or something." She never called him by anything other than his full name, and chastised me if I didn't use it, too.

Douchebag would do something like that. I didn't say it out loud, though, and closed the web browser. Laura'd get pissed at me if I'd called Jackie a douchebag. That was the last thing I wanted. We had plans I didn't want ruined. *Big* plans. "So ... we still on for tonight?"

Her face brightened before turning light pink. "Yeah. Mom and Dad will be gone by seven. I told them I was going to Haley's for a sleepover, so I have to leave first. I'll be back before eight, so come over then, okay?"

We spent the next half hour discussing our strategy. Laura's neighbors, the Hellmins, were old and nosey. They ratted us out two months before when I went over to watch a movie on her dad's bowling night, which happened to coincide with her mom's book club. Laura wasn't allowed to have anyone over when either one of her parents were out. She was grounded for a week, and I was banned for two. Our New Years evening required stealth. I needed to sneak into her house, and it seemed like it would be harder than sneaking her out. After ten minutes of debate, I agreed to Laura's overly complicated plan. I couldn't remember a single aspect after we hung up. I'd just have to wing it.

December 31st, 2013 7:59pm

Cool night air seeped through my jacket as I knocked on the door one minute before I was supposed to show up at Laura's house. Night killed the daytime desert heat that gave New Mexico a two-different-worlds feeling. I glanced around the neighborhood for spies, especially the Hellmins, but their curtains were closed. It wasn't the first time I'd come over when her parents weren't home, but it was the first time since we'd gotten busted, and the first time we'd planned on doing more than make out.

Laura pulled the door open, grabbed my arm, and yanked me inside.

"What the—"

"Shhh. The neighbors might see you," she said in a shout-whisper. Even in the dark, her strawberry hair glowed. "Why didn't you come in the back door?"

I laughed even though I'd been thinking virtually the same thing. "So a guy knocking on your front door is creepier than a guy sneaking through your backyard?"

She smacked my arm before snaking her hand along my coat sleeve, her fingers entangling with mine. Tugging me forward while she walked backward, her expression shifted from freaked out to sultry. "Come on," she said, leading me into the living room.

The house showed off her parents' combined wealth. The Flaggerts owned one of the biggest houses in Taos, second only to Jeena Stills, who spent most of her time in Hollywood starring in one crappy blockbuster after another. Laura's parents, though, were the two best surgeons in the area. Her father specialized in hearts, while her mother turned flesh into plastic. That's what Laura called it, anyway. I didn't see anything wrong with her mom's job; if people wanted to improve themselves, why not? Laura believed people were perfect in their imperfections.

She led me into the sunken living room, where she'd laid out a picnic of champagne and strawberries by a caramel-colored king-sized satin comforter with pillows. The oversized gas fireplace blazed, casting a warm glow over the makeshift bed. To the left of the fireplace, the mounted ninety-inch flatscreen TV showed an aquarium scene with clown fish swimming through coral. The realism was scary.

"First, I thought we'd watch a movie over ... there." She nodded toward her picnic spread.

I slid my jacket off, tossing it over the back of the couch. Laura smiled; I'd worn the oxford with blue stripes she insisted I buy. I reached out and rubbed my hands along her upper arms, pulling her gently to me. When we were toe to toe, I rested my forehead to hers.

"Nixon ..." Her voice broke.

I leaned in, my lips as close to hers as I could get without touching. "Whatever you want, it's yours."

Her arms snaked up my chest and around my neck, bringing me against her so air couldn't get between us unless we shared. Holy hell, were we sharing it. I wrapped my arms around her, lifting her off the ground for a brief moment. When I set her back on her feet, she broke the kiss and pulled me toward the comforter. Laura must have had only one thing on her mind. So did I.

December 31st, 2013 11:58pm

So, I thought Laura had one thing on her mind, but it took us three hours and forty-seven minutes to get there. Not that I counted. Contentment washed through me as I stared at the vaulted ceiling. Firelight glinted off the exposed beams above me.

She'd planned the entire evening out and wanted to stick with it. We even spent a good half an hour talking about Jackie's stupid obsession with that website. Laura couldn't access it at her house, even though she tried every search engine she knew of, and she knew a lot. Instead, she made me recite every word I could remember, which was pretty much the entire thing. I even impressed myself. I didn't mind; the end result between us was the same.

Laura's hand shifted on my bare chest, reminding me of what we'd done and filling me with emotions I'd never experienced or even thought possible. It wasn't just about getting laid, either. With Laura, it was special. Like she was meant to be my first. Maybe my only. I couldn't imagine anything better than the way she fit against me.

"It's almost midnight," she said, a tremble affecting her voice on the last word. She tugged the comforter closer to her chin.

I leaned back to glimpse the expression on her face, greeted by the top of her head and the still perfect part in her hair. "You okay?"

She nodded, a sniffle escaping.

Panic combusted the insides of my chest. *How can she be crying? You aren't supposed to cry after sex.*

I slid out from underneath her so we lay face to face. Her pale skin couldn't hide the fact she'd started crying even if she wiped away the evidence. She hid her eyes behind her hand. I reached out and tugged it gently away.

"Laura, look at me," I said, trying not to betray how much her tears killed me. We'd done it, and she started bawling. I didn't even think it was tear-inducing sex.

She met my stare, tears streaming down her cheeks.

"What's wrong?" I took over the job of wiping her cheeks using my thumb, a move most guys in chick flicks used.

"I ... I don't know." Her voice was just louder than the crackling of the fire. "I ..."

Her body wracked with more sobbing, and I pulled her to my bare chest. Everything had been perfect until she started crying. Laura had smiled at me after we'd done it. She'd told me she loved me a hundred times. None of that added up to equal a fit of tears.

I put my finger under her chin and tilted her head toward mine. Another move I'd seen in the movies. Girls loved that shit.

"Laura ..." I intentionally let her name linger as our gazes locked. With a small smile, I bent my head to hers and gently kissed her. A thrill filled me as she kissed me back.

Until she didn't.

Her lips turned hard and cold. The grandfather clock in the dining room struck midnight.

I jumped away from her. *What the hell?* "Laura?"

Laura looked like her usual angelic self, except for the fact that she wasn't moving. I shoved her shoulder; it would've been easier to move Pike's Peak.

"Laura? Laura!" I shouted her name ten—no, twenty times. Nothing changed. I tapped her cheek. Still nothing. Desperate for a reaction, I did the only thing I could think of, something I swore I'd never do: I slapped her face—a face like a Greek statue, solid and rock hard.

My hand pulsed in time with the hammering in my chest.

Panic pushed me to my feet. I scanned the room, trying to find anything that would give me a clue as to what happened, as sweat covered my forehead, making my hair stick to my skin. I glanced at the TV, where clown fish were frozen in their virtual swim.

A glitch in the program could've done that.

Turning to the fire, the flames were stuck in a macabre dance. I opened the grate and reached in, skimming my fingers over the top of the flames—albeit a stupid idea, but they didn't burn. A laugh escaped my lips as I curled my hand into the heart of the fire. There wasn't any heat to burn me. The fire, the TV, Laura—nothing moved except me.

I ran outside in my boxer briefs, the slap of my bare feet against the concrete echoing off the siding, and stopped in the middle of the driveway. A blanket of eerie silence filled the air. No birds, no cars, no people. Across the street, Mrs. Hellmin stood in the window, peering toward me with vacant eyes. Scary as that was, the worst part was the sky. No stars. No moon. Nothing but darkness.

I ran back into the house and stopped at Laura's frozen body.

A solid tick tick of the grandfather clock filled the room. I glanced over, and the hands of the clock continued to move.

Ten minutes after midnight. Why would time keep going, if nothing else did? Nothing else. Just the clock. Like a countdown.

The thirteenth month.

Son of a bitch. Jackson was right.

Day 1, 12:32am

After ten minutes of staring at that damned clock, I threw on the rest of my clothes and went into Laura's father's study. She'd once told me that he kept a handgun in his desk. Seemed like an idiotic place to keep a gun. I'd have kept it in my bedroom. I finally found it in the bottom right drawer.

After stuffing it in the waistband of my jeans, I ran out the front door with the barrel pressing into my lower back. Out of habit, I locked the door behind me, which seemed stupid, all things considered. Who was going to break into Laura's house when I was the only one walking around? I *was* the only one walking around, right? It couldn't be just a localized phenomenon around Laura's block.

My toes numbed as I stared at Mrs. Hellmin's frozen face in her window. What was really going down? Why was it happening to me?

What about Mom? Dad? Jackie? Were they stuck, too?

Maybe I'd fallen asleep. Maybe I'd landed in some kind of dream. That didn't seem right, either, but I clutched onto that hope before it floated away.

I had to figure out what the hell was going on, and a nagging voice that sounded a lot like my mother's told me the first place to go was home. It wasn't like there was a sign announcing my intended destination: 'Last Person on Earth? This is where you go!' I had to know my family was okay.

I jogged down the block to where I parked my rusted out Chevy Nova that was probably pretty cherry in its day. The scent of the old leather and stale foam comforted me for a moment. At least I had my car. I dug the keys out of my pocket and stuck them in the ignition. Taking a deep breath, I turned the key and waited for the roar of the engine.

Nothing happened.

I tried again and got the same result. Even though I knew it wasn't going to work, I kept turning the key. My frustration grew with each failed attempt, until I slammed my hands into the steering wheel so hard that it should've shook. It was as rock solid as Laura's body. Not in a good way.

That left me with one way home. My feet. Laura lived less than two miles from me, so I took off, sprinting most of the way. Somewhere in the back of my mind, it seemed stupid to be running. If the world was really frozen, what was the point? I had to check on my family, though.

No air moved, and by the time I was home, sweat dripped into my eyes. I stood outside the front door, not sure if I wanted to see the inside. Our house was a simple two-story with a two-car garage. The cream siding made it look like every other house on the block, but it had a different feel. It wasn't just a house; it was home.

I put my hand on the doorknob, surprised by the coolness of the metal. With a twist, I pushed it open and stepped inside. With my luck, my parents would be frozen in some kind of nasty embrace, like the time I caught them getting it on in the kitchen when I was ten. Not a moment to replay. Ever.

The only sound came from the sharp intake and exhale of my own breath. I climbed the steps slowly until I realized Mom wasn't going to bust me for sneaking in. A pang hit my gut. Her ear-shattering voice would've been welcome. Instead, she sat on the couch, frozen to her knitting needles, garish orange yarn clashing with the rest of the living room.

Dad sat in his recliner, remote in hand, with 'Nightly NewsLedger' on the screen. *No celebrating New Year's around our house when there's an election coming up.* My father's obsession with all things political was the stuff of legend. Hence mine and Jackson's names. Red, white, and blue decked out our living room with a giant American flag hanging on the wall above the couch. The entertainment center showcased election paraphernalia dating back to the sixties. The first time I brought Laura home, I was terrified she'd run out the door screaming. She surprised me by asking Dad questions and engaging him in a political debate about some bill in the state house. If I hadn't already been in love with her, that would've been the moment I fell.

Jackson sat on the floor with his legs stretched out and crossed at the ankles, an irritated expression cemented on his face. I snorted. *Frozen as the rest of the world. Oh, the irony.* He expected the apocalypse, and he was the one who would miss out. I'd take my virginity back to trade places with him.

The fact that he had been watching the same show as my father made me laugh. Jackie hated Dad's obsession with politics as much as I did. Plus, he always wanted to watch the ball drop in Times Square, and no doubt, Dad kept telling him he'd change the channel 'in a minute'. He'd done the same thing to me every year. The first time I saw the ball drop was when I was fourteen and at Melissa Speel's party. It was also the first night I touched a bra.

If they remained frozen, there'd be no more of Mom's bitching about the trash. No more of Dad's snoring in his recliner. No more of Jackson's conspiracies. No more, 'Nixon, what're you going to do with your life?' lectures from either one of my parents.

A dull ache settled in the pit of my stomach as a million memories rushed through my head. They say life flashes before the eyes when facing death. Mine flashed even though I lived, watching my family in what could be their final moments.

Unless I figured out whatever was going on, or someone fixed it.

I headed toward my room to change out of my sweaty clothes. As soon as I pulled on a fresh pair of jeans and my favorite T-shirt, the laptop beeped. The screen lit up, the cursor blinking in the password field. In two strides, I crossed the room and pulled out the chair, typing the password as I sat.

Thank God it works.

Hope pressed on my chest as the machine whirred to life.

Maybe I'm not alone. Maybe I'm just freaking out.

The screen faded to the website Jackie'd obsessed over. I stared at the countdown clock that flashed all zeros.

The thirteenth month.

My head dropped into my hands. The whole time I'd been pretending I was in some waking dream, it was real—not some imaginary game playing in my head during post-sex sleep. *The world is frozen. I am alone.*

The computer beeped again, and I jerked my head up.

The angel in the upper left was gone, and the other one stared at me with a creepy smile. Its evil eyes glared at me, and I was lost in the inferno again. A guttural voice rang in my head, repeating the words I'd read on the site earlier in the day. My body frozen—as still as the rest of the world; I couldn't shift my toes as I tried to push away from the desk.

A long pause came, while fire in the angel's eyes changed to a battle scene of two men fighting with swords on a green hill overlooking a fog-filled valley. The men looked to be even height, even weight, and could've been identical twins, with their long blond hair and carved-from-glass builds. A chill crept down my spine as one pierced the other.

Michael and Azrael will have the necessities of survival.

The voice spoke again, filling the inside of my head as if the words were my own.

They must battle to the death before the end of the thirteenth day. One must win, or all will die. Go forth. Fight for life. Die for life. Or suffer for eternity.

My gaze broke free of the angel's glare, but I didn't stop staring at him. The angel grew larger, breaking free of the fifteen-inch screen. A smile spread across his face as his form vaporized and merged with my body.

A burning sensation filled my body as the angel invaded me. When his face melted into mine, my entire body jerked back. My chair skidded across the floor and slammed into the wall behind me, cracking my head against the wall. My skin superheated as the pain in my head exploded like dynamite in a mountain. The tips of my fingers dug into the arm of the chair until it all ended, and I was left with a chill seeping into my bones. I stretched my legs and arms; my muscles groaned and lengthened.

What in the hell just happened to me? I stood, not knowing my next move, and trying not to freak out as I stared down at my hand, half-expecting it to glow or something; I watched too many sci-fi movies.

I have to find the other one. I have to kill someone.

The new entity inside me agreed and gave me an internal push toward the door, a need to seek out the other. It was as if I didn't have full control of my body. *Weird.*

Am I death or mercy? Who are Michael and Azreal?

The angel didn't answer.

I strode back to the computer, not really understanding why I was so damn calm. After hitting the enter button several times, I finally gave up. The computer was as dead as everything else. I slammed my hands on the desk.

Dammit! How in the hell do I find the one person I'm supposed to kill? My hands pressed on each side of the computer, supporting my weight as I contemplated my options. *It's not like I can get on a plane.* The coldness of my own words sent a chill down my spine. *How can I kill another human being?*

A shadow passed over me from behind. My body turned rigid, cold. I didn't move as my survival skills kicked in. The shadow stepped farther into the room and raised something up.

Faster than I've ever moved, I swung my leg behind me and kicked. A loud crack filled the room. I crouched into gedan position and stared my attacker in the face for the first time.

If life hadn't already been frozen, it would've stopped then and there.

Jackie stood before me with his left arm swinging beside his body at an awkward—definitely broken—angle, and Mom's butcher knife in his right hand. His brow furrowed, eyes tiny slits of rage, of hate.

I wanted to hug my brother, to celebrate that we weren't alone, but tears edged in my eyes as I reached toward him. Like a prison door banging shut in my mind, all emotions drained from me. I could see out, but I couldn't *get* out. I was still me, but the need to kill consumed me.

"I warned you this day was coming," he said in that creepy deep voice he'd used before. He raised the knife like a tomahawk. "Forgive me, brother," he said in a calm, calculated tone, and threw the blade. I dove onto the bed, pulling the nine-millimeter from my waistband. The knife stuck into the wall with a dull thud. Without hesitating, I pointed and pulled the trigger. I flinched, anticipating a loud band, but nothing happened.

A fleeting image flashed through my head. Me in a red uniform with a musket pointed at Jackie in tattered clothes. It had failed, too. How many times had we been in the same situation? Brother against brother?

"You should remember as well as I that gun powder doesn't work, brother." Jackie laughed as his face darkened.

With his left arm out of commission, I had my chance. Each possible move flicked through my mind like drawings in a notebook. I tossed the gun on the bed behind me as I leapt from the bed into gedan position. I had no doubt I could kill him by breaking his neck, but I had to get to him first. That meant going after his injured arm.

I swung around as Jackie slammed into me, his weight knocking me back onto the bed. Rage fueled his battle cry as he struck me in the face with his fist. Blood spurted from my nose and down my chin. I rammed my knee into his stomach and kicked out, throwing him off the bed.

Leaping from the mattress, I met him in the middle of the room. He blackened my eye as I jabbed and broke his nose. My body moved on instinct. I went after his left arm, but he kept it away from me, letting his right side take the brute force of my attack.

He blocked my second kick with his broken limb, the bone crunching again as my foot connected with his crushed arm. With his right hand, he jabbed my chest and knocked me back against his dresser, scattering his precious trophies. Jackie ran out the door with his left arm dangling at his side, blood spilling down his face.

I didn't chase him. My own wounds needed attention. I had gotten a few hits on him, but the war was far from over. We were still alive, and one of us couldn't survive.

The front door slammed shut, and I collapsed back onto my pillow. The fight took a lot out of me. Bruises from where Jackie hit me emerged and began to heal, but exhausted me further. The pain of each cracked knuckle rose to the surface like an air bubble beneath the churning sea.

I replayed each move I made and how he countered.

My little brother will be hard to defeat.

I had to *kill* my brother. The gate that locked down my emotions opened. Nausea turned me to my side, and I hurled the contents of my romantic evening with Laura onto the floor. When I was five and Jackie had his first birthday, I'd been so jealous of the attention he got that I threw his cake on the floor. When I was ten and Jackie fell in the neighbor's pool, I jumped in to save him as he stared wide-eyed at me from the bottom. When I was fourteen and broke my ankle, Jackie sat beside me in my room, reading comics with me. *So many great times.* No matter how much the little shit got on my nerves, I loved him.

I have no choice but to take his life.

Day 4, 7:05am

For three days I kept my eye out for Jackie. If it wasn't for the annoying ticking of the clock in my head, I wouldn't have known the day or time. My bruises were gone after I woke up two days ago, and although I was sure it would heal fast, I was pretty sure his broken arm would take longer to heal. Instead of pain easing away, my skin knitted together and pushed out the blood and damaged tissues. It hurt almost as bad as getting kicked in the balls. Accelerated healing sucked.

The quiet of the neighborhood pushed down on me. After a day and a half in my house, I had to get out. There wasn't anything at home I could use as a weapon except Mom's kitchen knives. Those might've done the job, but the image of the angels battling with swords stayed with me. I needed something significant to take my little brother down without leaving homebase too vulnerable.

It didn't help that, every time I thought of what I needed to do, guilt welled in my chest. How could I live with myself, if I did it? If I murdered my brother? Would I even remember?

On the fourth day of living hell, I walked into Ralph Parnum's house three blocks from mine. Ralph sat in the basement of his parent's house and played video games all day. His mom tried to kick him out before Thanksgiving, but his dad wouldn't let her. He said there was no way he was kicking his son out during the holidays. Or so I heard. Made a good story, if it was true.

I didn't expect much at Ralph's house and almost skipped it. There wasn't much on the first floor, and the second story was just as useless. I figured I'd try the basement, even though I only expected to see Ralph on a couch with a joint and a game controller in his hand.

Ralph's basement was a museum of swords. On the wall, three katanas and two samurai swords hung in frames with red velvet backgrounds. The bookshelf by the old big screen TV was filled with martial arts movies and books. There were also about twenty, or so, throwing stars in clear plastic boxes.

Sometimes being wrong pays off. Not that I was all that wrong.

In the middle of the half finished room, Ralph sat on an ugly flower sofa in front of the TV, with some martial arts game on the screen, and the joint was in an ashtray on the coffee table instead of his hand. I wondered if he was dealing but shook off the thought. It didn't matter. I had bigger issues than Ralph Parnum's illegal shit.

I grabbed the backpack I carried and unzipped it. Without bothering to open the boxes, I tossed all the throwing stars inside, noting most were six pointed while the rest had five. They could kill if thrown hard enough, but I knew that wasn't how I was going to take Jackie down. At best, they'd be a decent distraction. I'd have to use the swords like the vision the angel showed me. I set the bag down and pulled a wobbly chair beneath the katanas. The wider bladed samurai swords were too bulky for me, and wanting the thinner katanas, I yanked all three frames from the wall.

One sword balanced wrong in my hand, tilting too far to the left. The other two were perfect. I searched the basement for a way to carry them. In the closet I found several gun holsters, which seemed odd since I didn't find a single gun in the house. Digging through the mess, I discovered two shoulder straps. After adjusting them, I slid the swords into the spot for handguns. It wasn't ideal, but it wasn't bad, either.

Heading back up the stairs, I locked the basement door

behind me and pocketed the key, in case Jackie was doing the same thing. He wouldn't be able to get to the other swords unless he broke down the door.

When I got back to the house, I pulled out one of the swords and checked each room. Mom and Dad hadn't moved. *Obviously.* Every room in the house was empty otherwise. I tossed my newly acquired weapons on the table, taking each throwing star out of its box.

They didn't even break my skin when I touched them. The katanas had been sharpened and polished, but the throwing stars would bounce off cotton candy, if I used them. Grabbing Mom's knife sharpeners from the drawer, I set to work.

The project set my mind at ease as the constant motion worked my muscles into a dull ache. The need to get the stars ready was all I focused on. For that moment, I forgot why I was sharpening blades, why I needed the stars. It was a sort of meditative trance, and I welcomed it. For the last four days, I'd only thought about Jackie and what I had to do.

I finished just past noon and ate the bread I'd taken from Jenna Miller's house the day before, and drank my last bottle of water. Apparently, the necessities of survival the angel mentioned meant nothing but bread and water. Everything else I tried to eat had been like a rock. That alone was enough for me to leave the house and start hunting.

Something nagged me as I strolled down the street. If I died, would I come back to life once time started, or would I stay dead? One of us would keep life the same. The other would change it. Who did what? If I killed Jackie, would life start back the same, or different? Would I wake up next to Laura in her living room? Or would I even exist? Too many questions.

I turned into the Shady Buttes Mall parking lot, not realizing I'd walked so far or for so long. The lot was oddly empty of people, but plenty of cars filled the spaces. As I stalked closer to the cinema entrance, I could see that a movie had let out just before the world stopped. The lobby was crowded, Jenny Meyrick among them with her head thrown back in a laugh. I recognized several other kids from my class, too. Laura and I should've been with them. The image of her frozen face, covered in tears, flashed in my mind. I should've checked on her. I should've seen that she was okay.

Guilt wrecked my concentration. It wasn't until I was at the entrance to the stores that the prison door slammed my emotions shut again, and I realized someone followed me.

Jackie was somewhere behind me, but I didn't know where. Goosebumps spread up my neck as a creepy feeling of being watched sent a shiver up my back. The only thing I could do was keep going. I pulled one of the throwing stars out of my belt.

My mind locked onto his location, followed by each of my senses. His cheap cologne mixed with sweat filled my nose like he was in front of me. Twenty paces behind and to my left, his soft footfalls echoed in my ears. It was like I had eyes on the back of my head; I could see everything around me. He darted ahead of me, crouching low enough between cars to hide his face but not his blond hair. I turned toward the street but slowed my steps.

When I was ten paces from his hiding spot, he leapt out with his own sword. I threw the star with a skill I didn't know I had. Jackie twisted to the side as the star sliced through his shirt. I drew both katanas as he rushed me.

Metal clashed, echoing off the building. Jackie's training in tae kwon do usurped my instincts. He thrust, jabbed, and slashed, while it took all my strength to block his attacks. He was faster than I'd ever seen him move. The tip of his single sword sliced at my skin, while mine never got near him. There was no doubt in my mind that he'd win the fight if I kept in it, especially as my muscles weakened with each blow I blocked. He swept up with the sword, the tip catching along my cheek, carving a line upward into my scalp.

The burning in my arms was nothing compared to the pain in my face.

Jackie slashed my chest before I could recover. In one swift move, Jackie sent both of my katanas flying out of my hands to clatter against the concrete sidewalk. Jackie laughed in bursts between heavy breaths. He brought the sword above his head.

I jumped toward him, knocking him into a truck, and slammed my fist into his kidneys as hard as I could. His strength gave under my assault, and I hit him three more times. The sword fell from his hands, slicing a thin curved line down my back.

I pushed him to the ground and ran for my life.

Jackie's laughter echoed in my ears. "You never were good with a sword."

Day 6, Time unknown

I woke in the basement of Ralph Parnum's house. The mini-fridge was empty except for one bottle of water, which I downed in four gulps. Crawling on my knees, I slid beneath the gray cotton comforter I'd dragged from his parents' bedroom. Within seconds, I blacked out.

Day 7, 8:46am

Sweat and blood weighed my clothes down when I woke the next day. The wounds were mostly healed, with the exception of the slice in my left arm. Jackie'd nearly cut me to the bone. Once I'd run from the fight, I knew home would be the first place he'd search. The katanas were lost, either in the parking lot or to my brother, leaving me with only a few throwing stars that wouldn't do much against Jackie's arsenal. That left me with Ralph's house. The unbalanced katana remained, and it would have to do until I could find something else. Plus the basement was secure, and Jackie'd never look for me at Ralph's.

I pulled my shirt off as I sat up. The floor hadn't been an ideal place to sleep, but it was the best hiding place—just in case Jackie did break down Ralph's basement door. My jeans weren't as bad, so those stayed in place. Shirtless, I strode across the length of the house to the small bathroom I'd seen the first time I walked down the steps.

Of course, the water wouldn't turn on, but the toilet tank held more than enough to clean the blood off my skin. I stared at myself in the mirror, my face gaunt and dark circles ringing my eyes. My cheekbones stuck out farther than usual. I looked like a zombie who hadn't eaten in way too many days. In reality, it was kind of true. All I'd had since time stopped was water and bread. I'd have given anything for a prime rib and baked potato. Even a burger and fries. Pizza. Milkshake. Just the idea of them made my mouth water.

My stomach grumbled. Food and water meant leaving the safety of the basement. I climbed the steps and pressed my ear against the door. *Please don't let Jackie be here,* I begged to no one. Nothing sounded in the eerie quiet. With the katana firmly in hand, I twisted the doorknob.

My stomach churned from hunger and fear. I needed food, but the nagging terror ate into my starvation. I inspected each room, twice raising my sword when I thought I saw movement. The shadows seemed to sway, echoing my own motions. The pounding of my heartbeat displaced the quiet.

I dug into the breadbox in the kitchen, devouring an entire loaf. The bread weighed on my stomach, and my paranoia heightened. I drained two bottles of water from the upstairs fridge, too. With the walls closing in around me, I ran out the door, not caring if Jackie'd meet me. I had to get out of the damned house.

Stale air filled my lungs, expanding my chest and breaking the invisible constrictions that gripped me. The ocean sound that had begun in my ears before I fled abated. Peace settled over me. It calmed my heart and my mind. Glancing over my shoulder at the house, I realized my own mind had trapped me inside. Seven days without another human being. Seven days and the only person to talk to wanted to kill me. Seven days.

Six more to go.

New Year's Eve at Laura's house seemed like a lifetime ago. I had to see her, to know she was okay. There wasn't any reason to think she wasn't, but the need consumed my mind. I ran, blood pumping through my heart and filling my ears. There wasn't any reason to run other than the desperation to know.

My shoulder slammed into her front door as I tried to open it. In my rush, I'd forgotten I'd locked it. I went around back and checked the sliding glass door. It slid open with ease. The kitchen glowed from the soft light that hung over the sink and illuminated the way to the living room.

Nothing had changed, not that I expected it to.

I sat between the fireplace and Laura's partially covered body.

Her eyelids were half-closed with tears clinging to the corners, forever frozen in an agony I didn't understand. I reached out to wipe the edges of her eyes and cut my thumb on the glasslike tears, leaving a thin trail of blood across her cheek.

Sobs racked my body as the weight of the last several days broke me until the snot and tears wouldn't come anymore. My chest burned as the stale oxygen filled my lungs. I couldn't even feel the soft touch of my girlfriend when I needed it the most.

"I have to kill my brother, Laura," I whispered to her still-frame. "Jackson has to die for us to be together again. For the world to start again. For . . . everything." I imagined her wrapping her arms around me. "How am I supposed to do it?"

I stared at her prone body, wishing for an answer and knowing none would come.

"What will I remember?" Sighing, I moved closer and lay beside her. Just being close to her made me feel a little better, though Laura should have been soft, warm against my skin, not like a steel beam exposed to a winter wind. I slid my hand against hers. My heart opened, and the events of the thirteenth month spilled from my lips. I let everything out of my system, feeling lighter, freer, the more I talked.

The day slipped by, and I knew I had to leave her. Talking to Laura had eased my burden but hadn't changed anything. I still had to kill my brother. After kissing her cheek, I left her behind once again and headed toward my hideout, breaking into houses on the way.

I broke into Ralph's neighbor's house, without a clue as to what I'd find, and wished I hadn't. While exploring the house, I found the owners in their bedroom doing what Laura and I had done. Only stuck like that.

Not something I wanted to see.

Especially with wrinkles.

The kitchen was stocked with Italian, French, and sourdough bread. There were four refillable water bottles tucked in the back of the fridge. I stuffed everything in my backpack with the throwing stars. Even though I doubted there'd be anything useful in the rest of the house, Ralph's had surprised me, so maybe his neighbors would have, too.

I opened the door of the home office in the basement, where a gun cabinet stood in the corner behind a desk. The things people hid in their basements surprised me. I dug into the cabinet and uncovered a large hunting knife. It gleamed in the hallway light. I attached the sheath to my belt and kept looking, but found nothing else that could help.

For the rest of the day, I searched other houses. In the end, I discovered one more hunting knife, but no other weapons.

I was as good as dead. The only consolation was it would be over. I just didn't know in what way. No matter what, I needed to win. My gut told me that needed to be the outcome if life was to continue as it was before. I was the one who could achieve that.

With renewed determination, I went back to Ralph's house, headed to the basement and cleared off the unused ping-pong table. Scenes from movies flashed in my mind. Generals always had a plan. Granted, I was my own army, but that didn't mean I couldn't try to figure out the best course of action.

My body was still healing, and I was in no condition to hunt Jackie. I needed to rest, to think, to plan. There had to be a way to win.

There had to be a way to kill my brother.

Day 13, 10:33am

Silence woke me. I sat up, waiting for a bird or the sound of the shower running. For thirteen days, I kept hoping I would wake from my walking nightmare. Any noise would've been welcomed after so much quiet. Except the one I heard.

The image from the website returned on Ralph's big screen TV.

At the end of the thirteenth year, death and mercy will meet during the thirteenth month to determine the course of humanity. Time will stop. Life will cease until one dies.

If death wins, life continues.

If mercy wins, life changes.

If neither defeats the other before the end of the thirteenth day of the thirteenth month of the thirteenth year, life ends.

Michael and Azrael will have the necessities of survival. They must battle to the death before the end of the thirteenth day. One must win, or all will die. Go forth. Fight for life. Die for life. Or suffer for eternity.

It took all my strength not to shout 'no shit!' at the top of my lungs.

Your time is up. You must finish the war, or lose everything.

That was new. A light flashed on the TV, and the screen shifted from the frozen video game to the countdown clock from the website. It displayed hours. Thirteen left.

Time was up.

Day 13, 5:11pm

After napping and eating what had to be my last meal of bread and water, I walked toward Mason Memorial Park. Had time continued to move, the sun should have disappeared beneath the horizon. Had time continued, I would have been back in school, taking classes with Laura and planning my future. Had time continued, I might have felt like myself. I didn't know when I stopped being me, but somewhere along the way I became someone else. I became a fighter. A warrior.

I wanted to be the boy who called his brother a douche and thought only of being with his girlfriend.

That Nixon was gone.

Mason Memorial Park was the largest park in our suburb and named after the man who'd sold the land to the city. On our second date, Laura and I had picnicked beneath a massive oak tree near the playground. The image of her frozen face covered in tears flashed in my mind. I should've checked on her one last time.

I knew Jackie would be around. Though, the park was big enough that it might be hours before we found one another. I listened for movement even in the deafening quiet. Without wind or birds or people, the silence was absolute. I was careful not to be the one to give away my position. My sensei taught us how to keep control of our bodies, so each step, each movement, couldn't be heard. Years of training had finally come in handy.

After an hour of walking through the wooded area, I emerged by the same playground where Jackie jumped off the slide, when he was ten, and sprained his wrist. The image of his face, as he prepared to bring the sword down on me, flashed in my mind. It wasn't the blond-haired angel Mom loved who'd tried to kill me; he was ugly in that moment. Like me, something had changed him. I would not fight my brother but a stranger in my brother's skin.

A crack, like a gunshot, rang out to my left. Jackie didn't waste time rushing at me with a feral yell.

Our swords clashed and rang, metal on metal, into the forever night sky. The lights of the park reflected off his sweat-covered frame. Again like me, he gave up wearing a shirt.

For twenty minutes, by my internal clock, we didn't speak. Our swords and our grunts were the only sounds in the park. Jackie brought his sword overhead and swung it down, meeting my katana. It took more strength than I had to shove him off of me. He stumbled backward and fell onto his ass.

I leapt toward him, but he kicked out with his left foot and slammed it into my stomach. All the air rushed from my lungs as the burning lack of oxygen brought me to my knees.

"Well played, brother," Jackie said between hacking coughs.

I rolled onto my heels. "What happened to us, Jackie?"

He laughed as he struggled to his feet. "You really don't know, do you? Who we are? What we're meant to do? Even after suffering through it, you have tried to hold on to Nixon."

"I am Nixon," I said as I stood. My stomach cramped, making it hard to stand straight.

Jackie smiled and the image of the angels from the website came to me.

"I *am* Nixon," I said again, as if that would make it true. I knew without a doubt who he thought he was, who he thought I was. "We're no angels."

"That's where you're wrong," he said with a blank face.

He swung his sword out from his left, slicing into my shoulder before I could move out of the way. I fell to my knees, dropping my blade. Hot blood spilled from the gaping wound in my shoulder, covering my chest in a matter of seconds. I tried to lift my arm, but the command from my brain went unnoticed. I couldn't risk glancing down to see how bad it really was.

Jackie stood over me with a smile on his face. "When will you learn? This is not your fight to win, brother. It's your fight to lose."

His lips twitched into a sneer as he glared down at me. I didn't let him out of my sight as I slid my right hand under my left arm and unsheathed the hunting knife. I writhed in pain, both fake and real, as I yanked the knife out.

"We should've just finished this on day one. Instead, we take it to the thirteenth day every single time." Jackie shook his head. My ignorance must have shown on my face. "You really don't remember, do you? And here, I've been thinking you were faking it the entire time."

I can fake a lot of things, but even this is a bit much.

"Usually, the memories have come to you by the final day, or so you've always told me. Maybe this time is a little different. No matter." He raised the sword above his head with a glint of glee in his eyes. "The end result is always the same."

He yelled at the same time I did. As his sword swung toward my skull, my knife headed toward his stomach. I pushed forward, slamming the blade into his gut. The bloodcurdling scream that tore from his lips rang in my ears as I lifted the knife upward, deepening the blade and ensuring the death blow was mine. His blood flowed down my arm, pooling in the crook of my elbow before slipping off my skin.

The sword fell from his hands, and the hilt bounced off my shoulder harmlessly.

Jackie collapsed on top of me. I pushed him off with my good arm, laying him on his back. Blood poured from the hole in his stomach and through his fingers. His eyes began to glaze over as I stood over him. I held his head up with my good arm and stared back at my little brother, memories rushing in again. Tears slid free as I pushed the past away.

The thirteenth month would end in a matter of minutes. With any luck, I wouldn't remember gutting Jackie when the world started again, but would I remember him at all? Would he even be there once the nightmare ended?

"You finally did it." His voice came out scratchy and raw. Tilting his head to his right, he spit out a mouthful of blood. "The world will change, Michael. You've finally defeated me. Everything will change now."

"Azrael?" His name dropped onto my tongue without a thought behind it.

He smiled, teeth covered in his blood. "You do remember." He closed his eyes and weighed heavy in my arm. "From today forward, you will remember everything. That is the burden of winning. That is the burden of changing the world."

If death wins, life continues. If mercy wins, life changes. I am Michael, the angel of mercy. I've just changed the world.

Azrael, Jackie, my brother, coughed and went still.

I will never forget.

January 1st, 2014 7:00am

A hand shoved my shoulder.

"Get up. They're coming," a high-pitched voice said in my ear. "Hurry, please. You know what'll happen if you don't get up."

I sat forward onto my elbows, hitting my head on something above my bed. *That's not right.* Rubbing the forming knot, I stared at the bottom of a bunk bed.

Since when do Jackie and I have bunk beds?

"Jackie," a deep feminine voice came from the hallway. "Is Eleanor up yet?"

Who the fuck is Eleanor?

"Yes, Mama." The voice hitched on the last 'a', like my brother's often did, only softer and half an octave higher.

That's not right, either. I turned to stare into the blue eyes of a blonde-haired girl—the image of a Renaissance cherub. Her eyes were wide.

"Jackie?" I asked, croaking at the sound of my own voice. "What's going on?"

Her eyes grew a fraction wider. "The movement. Remember? Today's the day they come for you. To take you to the new colony."

The past rushed in on me and merged with the reality of what stood before me. My brother, Jackie, my mother and her knitting needles. My father with his political talk. They mixed with my sister, Jackie, my mother in her gray skirt, stirring broth for dinner, and my father in a military uniform that marked him as a lowly guard. The thirteenth month. The knife cutting into Jackie's belly spilling his blood. Jackie's warning that I would remember everything.

I sat up, slamming my head once again into the bunk above me. Instead of a spacious bedroom with two twin beds, two desks, and crap everywhere, I was in a drab gray prison cell with a door, and a slim window that let in just enough sunlight that I could see Jackie.

The life I knew was gone.

I was about to ask who Eleanor was when I looked down. Gone was the thin, athletic male frame. In its place, I had a well-endowed female body.

Oh, my God, I'm Eleanor.

My stomach clenched, and I doubled over. Everything that had happened to Nixon was still in my mind, even the battle in the thirteenth month, Jackie's laughter at my stupid jokes, his shock when I shoved the knife into his stomach, and the feel of Laura's hands on my back. Every memory of Eleanor's life was there, too. Growing up in a small cubicle on the eightieth floor of an apartment town. Going to school with the rest of the residents in our building on the fifth floor. Never walking outside because there wasn't anywhere to walk. The buildings were so close nobody could squeeze between them. Never playing in the grass, because there wasn't any grass anymore. Or trees. The world was entombed in a sphere to maintain the Earth's atmosphere. I remembered everything from both of my lives.

A small mirror beside the door reflected the light from the window on the opposite of the wall. I stood before it, combing my fingers through my long, brown hair. Nixon's eyes stared back at me. My cheekbones were higher, more feminine, but I looked the same. Me with boobs.

Life continued without death.

The world was overpopulated to the point that the skies were filled, and the last place uninhabited by humanity was the sea.

I was part of the movement to create the first colony beneath the waters off the Pacific Ocean.

Mom didn't greet me or say her goodbyes as Jackie walked me out the door and to the elevator. The stark gray walls damped my mood more. How had I gotten myself into such a mess?

"I should've let you kill me," I whispered, more to myself than my sister.

Jackie raised an eyebrow. "What're you talking about?"

I shook my head and stared at myself in the silver elevator doors. The part of me that was still Nixon thought, 'I'd do me.' I stifled the laugh that bubbled in my throat.

"I'm going to miss you, Ellie." Jackie wrapped her arms around me.

"Me, too." I almost added, "I'll visit soon," but that would have been a lie. I wouldn't. I'd never see my sister or the inside of my building again. I'd never see the surface. Once I was in the colony, I would stay there.

The doors dinged and opened. Nobody waited for me. With a quick glance at my sister, I stepped inside. For the first time in Eleanor's life, I pushed the button to the ground floor. I'd never been lower than the girls' schoolrooms on the fifth. Tears welled in my eyes as I clutched my small bag closer to my chest.

At the twentieth floor, the elevator stopped and the doors slid open. A boy with strawberry blond hair stood on the other side. His eyes widened. The only boys I ever saw lived on my floor and were like my brothers.

"*Laura.*" Nixon spoke in my head.

I scooted into the corner so he could enter. He stepped to the opposite side, glancing down toward me several times as the elevator doors closed.

"I'm . . ." he said with a slight quiver. My heart lurched into my chest. The voice was deeper, but it was the same. "Have we met before?"

I shook my head and moved closer, offering my hand. "I'm Eleanor."

"Lorne." He touched my hand and electricity shot up my arm. He held on, the heat building between us. "Are you going to the Pacific colony?"

I could only nod.

"Are you sure we haven't met before? I feel like … like I know you, somehow." He stepped closer, our hands still together. "Like I've known you forever."

My breath caught in my throat. Laura had told Nixon the same thing the first night he kissed her. If only Lorne knew what I knew. If he really was my Laura. The confusion of being Nixon and Eleanor cramped my stomach. I fell forward into Lorne. His warm hands caught me against him, and it reminded me so much of my last night with Laura. She was gone. Lorne wasn't really her, just a male version. Nixon needed her. Who did I need?

He held me as I wept and my heart ached. By killing my brother, I'd destroyed the world.

Nobody knew it but me. I alone must live with the truth.

By showing everyone mercy, I let everyone live, even when death should've come. Jackie had been right. I was meant to lose the battle.

One hundred years. That's how long I'd have to wait to fix what I did. How long I'd have to wait to die again during the thirteenth month.

Next time, I won't take it to the thirteenth day.

Acknowledgements

Thanks to Anastasia Ely, Jonathan Schkade, and Cory Herndon for their wonderful notes to make this story stronger. A HUGE shout out to J.A. Belfield, one of my favorite authors, who took the time to chat me through the story as I sorted things out. Thanks to the team at J. Taylor Publishing, for seeing Nixon's potentional and mine as well. I can't leave out the two most important people in my life, Bean and Dave. Without them, I wouldn't be who I am. I really am lucky.

L.S. Murphy

L.S. Murphy lives in the Greater St. Louis area where she watches Cardinals baseball, reads every book she can find, and weaves tales for young adults and adults. When not doing all of the above, she tends to her menagerie of pets as well as her daughter and husband.

Her debut novel Reaper is available now.

Sleepless Beauty

Kimberly Kay

J. Taylor Publishing

I didn't realize anything was wrong until I found the princess out cold on the floor.

"Shoot." I knelt at her side, nudging back her extravagant lace sleeve to check her pulse. Her heartbeat pattered under my fingertips.

Not caring if I soiled my gown, I crawled around to her head. As a palace servant, dirt *always* clung to me—something Princess Clarissa never failed to note. If conscious, she'd say something like, 'Are you cleaning the floor, Aesira, or is the floor cleaning you?'

A fair question but one I despised none-the-less.

I pushed Clarissa's long blonde hair off her face, half amazed the weight of her luscious locks hadn't suffocated her.

Fingers pressed against her forehead, I found no fever. I lifted one eyelid, staring into the hollow blue orb before waving my hand in front of it. No reaction. Her lid sprang back into place as I let go.

A soft blush crept over her cheeks while plush lips puckered as if expecting a kiss in her sleep.

"Shoot." I sat up straight, my long brown braid slapping my back. "Please tell me you weren't that stupid."

I raised her hand. On her index finger glistened a bead of ruby blood. Reaching for her other arm, I tugged the hem of her sleeve back to reveal the spindle she held.

"You *are* that stupid! Oh, no!" Sitting back, I ran my palms over my cheeks, surely leaving trails of dirt behind. Not that I cared at that moment, or ever.

Everyone knew of the curse cast on Clarissa when a baby—that she would prick her finger on a spindle before her eighteenth birthday and drop into a hundred-year sleep. The wicked witch did it because Clarissa's parents forgot to invite the hag to a fancy dinner, or something.

Not only was Clarissa cursed, but when she pricked her finger, the rest of her kingdom—including me—would be doomed to fall into our own kind of sleep. Not the same as Clarissa's—no, that would have been too kind of a wicked witch. Instead, when the sun set, we'd freeze—walking, cleaning, sleeping. *Anything. Anywhere.* Worse, we'd still be conscious—aware of our situation for a hundred years, or until Clarissa awoke.

Unfair. Just because of one stupid princess—or one witch's bad attitude—we'd all be stuck as living statues.

With a moan, I tugged the end of my braid. Clarissa pricking her finger at least explained why I felt so lethargic. I'd thought I was just extra tired as I dragged myself out of bed to do my chores, but it was truly the beginnings of the curse.

I glared down at Clarissa. "You're birthday is *tomorrow*! Why couldn't you hold off, huh? Spoiled, rotten—" I cut myself off. It's not that I hated Clarissa. Just because we were the exact same age with different circumstances didn't mean she deserved my enmity. I can't say pleasure tingled through me at the idea of remaining seventeen for the next hundred years, though.

Will I remain seventeen, or will I grow old and die while just sitting around?

Trying not to gag, I pushed myself to my feet.

No, there's a way out.

Every curse could be undone. I needed to remember how to resolve the one we'd fallen under. I'd heard the stories, but since I was only a baby when the princess had been cursed, stories were all I had. Even though with most stories I found it difficult to keep track of all the details, I was sure with the right motivation—saving the entire Kingdom, perhaps—I'd remember.

Pacing, I whispered to myself, saying, "'Upon the princess pure and small, a curse is cast to affect all. Come eighteen years …' Um … 'come eighteen years on spindle fair this kingdom's only heir …' Um … Something about getting pricked, and … 'asleep she'll fall. Her people, when sun sets, will wait a hundred years for her to wake. As living statues they'll …' Remain? And something about Clarissa's reign … 'To right what has been made amiss, all you need is … is …' Um …" I screwed my eyes closed. "'Is true love's kiss!' That's it!"

Would a kiss from Clarissa's tall, dark, handsome boyfriend, Edwin, the prince of the tiny Kingdom of Alacrity do the trick? Sure, they'd broken up last week—that gossip flew all over the castle faster than Clarissa could blush—nothing new. They broke up and got back together every other month. It made all of us dizzy; almost as dizzy as Ben made me.

My stomach did loop-de-loops at the mere thought of him, and my eyelids snapped open.

Oh, no! Ben!

Ben, with his hazel eyes overshadowed by a fringe of pale brown hair.

You can't let yourself think about him! I stared hard at Clarissa, whose golden locks spilled all over the stone floor, curling around the pink waistline of her dress as she snored. *Find a way to help your mistress. You should have prevented the curse from ever happening.*

Well, I wanted to say to myself, *it isn't* my *fault she has more curiosity than brains.* Besides, finding Edwin *would* help. If I rode a horse, I could reach Alacrity before noon. I'd drag Prince Edwin back by sunset, and it wouldn't take much to convince him to kiss her. They'd made out enough in the past that I knew she wouldn't mind. She'd probably even get back together with her charming prince—like usual.

I gathered my green skirts and fled the castle. Was I running slower than usual? *Should I warn the others? Ask them to move the princess?* What would be the point? I'd only incite panic. Besides, if things went my way, I'd fix the problem before it fully set in. People didn't even *need* to know Clarissa pricked her finger. I'd save the kingdom; she'd save face. Most importantly, I wouldn't be executed for letting the curse happen.

I skidded to a stop just inside the stable door, the scent of hay, oats, and manure smacking me full on in the face. "Tommy?" I gagged. "Tommy?"

"What, Aesira?" His voice drifted from the loft above.

I held my nose as I stepped further inside. It took a moment for my eyes to adjust to the darkness. "I need you to help me saddle the princess's horse. It's urgent."

His face appeared over the rim of the loft. Bits of hay fell to the floor—barely missing my head. "Cantchua do it yerself?"

I released my nose to put my hands on my bony hips. "Cantchua do yer own job fer once?" Usually, my impression of his accent riled him up.

Instead his head disappeared. "I don't much feel like movin'." The drawl slid out at the speed of molasses. "Yeh know? It's kinda funny. I don't feel tired, but I can't seem to make myself move fast neither."

The curse. It was as if one of the colts kicked my heart.

"Tommy! Get down here, and help me!" My voice sounded shriller than usual, coated as it was in fear.

He yawned almost as loudly as Clarissa had been snoring. "Do it yourself..."

I clenched my fists, kicking the fallen hay. *It's nothing,* I tried to tell myself. *Tommy is always lazy—even on his best days. Besides, the curse wouldn't put him to sleep. That's only Clarissa. The curse affects the rest of us by slowing us down.*

No matter what I told myself, I couldn't calm the anxiety throwing a party in my heart.

I ran to the stall of Clarissa's white mare. After a quick glance over my shoulder, I undid the bolt.

The mare stared at me with large, liquid brown eyes. Her pink lip drew back from her teeth as she made a sound I would label as 'growl' if it came from something that wasn't supposed to thrive off grass.

"You don't scare me." The shake in my voice made my words sound less convincing aloud than in my head.

With a snort, her ears flattened.

I took a step away. Could horses smell fear?

The mare tossed her head, doing a pretty good imitation of Clarissa as she turned her rump to me.

"Oh, come *on!*" I yelled to the world at large. "Won't *anyone* help me?"

"Help yerself..." Tommy said from above before a snore interrupted.

I glared at the loft. I glared at the stable. I glared at the mare. I hated horses. *Large, smelly, stupid beasts.* However, I would never make Alacrity on foot before the curse claimed me, too. I didn't want to even imagine how it would happen—how I'd move slower and slower until I just stopped.

I took a running leap onto the mare's broad back.

With a neigh, the horse reared, hooves clicking against the wall as her head brushed the ceiling. The only thing I heard over her scream was my own as she bolted from the stable.

She raced through the cobblestoned courtyard, hooves ringing. With a snort, and before I'd gathered my wits enough to close my mouth, she leapt over the drawbridge. People dove out of the way as we tore through the town square, upsetting a wagon of cabbages.

"Sorry!" I yelled over my shoulder to the poor, frantic man collecting his goods.

I clung to the mare's creamy mane in an attempt to both stay mounted and keep those silky locks of hers from slapping my face with every other step. *I hate horses!*

Farmsteads replaced houses, which in turn gave way to large fields as we galloped from the kingdom I'd never left before. My family had served the royal's for as long as I could count—back through the generations. Served them with grace and honor. Just my luck Clarissa wreaked havoc on her kingdom while *I* attended her.

Moron.

In the distance, the topmost spire of Alacrity's castle twisted into the sky. There I'd find Prince Edwin, and Ben.

Don't think about him. I closed my eyes. *It'll never work between you two. Just stop.*

Yet, with my eyes squeezed closed, I saw him clearly sitting next to me as his hand reached up to brush a tear off my cheek.

I yanked my eyes open to stare at the castle again. It was hard *not* to think about Ben when nothing else demanded my attention. Besides my impending doom.

Was the mare galloping slower? Her legs pumped in the same rhythm as before, covering the same distance, yet the grass we passed didn't blur with our speed. Instead, I saw each individual frond—as if we attempted to swim against a powerful current.

Foam glistened on her neck as we approached the edge of Alacrity, yet our movements were like flying through syrup—or running on sand.

At last I pulled back on the mare's mane. She glided to a stop, sides heaving, each breath sliding out on a sigh.

My own breath came out no better.

I reached up, intending to rub the mare's neck, but my hand didn't move with the speed I'd intended. I tried harder. It took almost a minute for my fingers to touch the horse's sweaty coat.

"Oh, no." It took me another minute to get those two words out.

The curse.

I dismounted—or rather, I fell off in slow motion. By the time I finally hit the ground, it couldn't hurt, and didn't.

Turning my head—which took what seemed like a century—I found a little boy staring at me with wide eyes. He'd dropped the toy boat he'd been holding but didn't seem to notice.

"Fetch the prince," I said in the same commanding tone the princess always used with me. Only it sounded more like "Feeeeetcccccch ... theeeeeeeee ... Priiiinceeeeee." My voice emerged strangely low, as if the words were squeezed from my gut instead of spoken like a normal human being.

The kid ran off without another word. He probably thought I was crazy. Worst of all, he probably wouldn't come back.

What could I do about it? The mare still breathed deep, as if trying to catch her breath, but she wasn't going to catch up to it anytime soon. As I stood, I breathed at the same pace. Every minute crawled by as I waited. Would someone else come along? Could I convince anyone to help me find the prince?

The whinnying of horses startled me—or would have if I could jump. My reaction looked like a shrug by the time I finished. I turned to find the child running ahead of a carriage with the royal seal of a rabbit stamped on its side. A scrawny servant sitting atop the coach yanked back on the reins. All six white horses stuttered to a stop.

I thought about shouting "Hooray!" except it would take forever. Instead, I clasped my hands as the door flew open. In a display of bravado and splendor, the prince stepped out, black hair gleaming. His silver cloak flared behind him as he thrust it backwards and used the same arm to point to the sky as he asked, "Where is the maiden that seeks my aid?"

Distracted, I stared past Prince Edwin at the hazel-eyed young man dressed in the red garb of one of Alacrity's servants. I turned away just as the little kid who had dropped the boat pointed at me, his mouth as wide open as when I'd last seen him.

The prince glanced past me several times before his gaze met mine. "Oh." His lips rumpled as his brows sank over his emerald eyes. "It's you. You can tell Clarissa she blew it. She lost her chance! We are never ever, *ever* getting back together." He spun around and lifted one leg onto the lowest carriage step.

"Curse." The one word would act as the quickest way to get my meaning across, even though it took forever for me to say it. I winced, which seemed to take half a century.

Prince Edwin stood more frozen than I did. At last, he turned back around. His chiseled chin hung as slack as the child's. "Excuse me?" His voice lifted three octaves on the last word.

Did he honestly want me to repeat myself? It would take *ages*. My gaze slid past him—to his personal servant.

Ben's mouth formed a thin line as he pushed away his fringe

of hair. He coughed once. "Prince, I believe Aesira's trying to say Clarissa's curse has come upon them."

Edwin's brows rose again. "I thought that was just a rumor. I mean, sure! When I broke up with her she threatened to prick herself, but I didn't think it would do anything more than appease her inner drama queen."

I stared at him. The urge to barf crawled up my throat. Clarissa seriously pricked her finger—risking the lives of everyone in her kingdom—to get even with her boyfriend?

"Anyway ..." Prince Edwin flashed a dazzling smile. Too bad the mere sight of him made me want to slap him upside the head. "What do you want me to do about it?" he asked.

Did he really want me to talk again? "True ... Love's ..."

Edwin flung out his arms. "Why are you talking so slow? I haven't got all day!"

Too bad the curse held me captive, or I *would* smack him upside the head. "Kiss ..."

Behind Edwin, Ben stiffened. In his eyes, I saw how he longed to help me. I knew him so well we could speak thousands of words with a single glance.

Gratitude seeped through me—that the blush climbing my cheeks rose so slowly neither man would likely notice it.

Edwin turned to Ben. "What is she trying to say?"

Ducking his head and hiding his eyes, Ben said, "Legend has it, Princess Clarissa's curse can only be broken by true love's kiss. Otherwise, Clarissa is doomed to sleep for a century, and the people of her kingdom will be frozen in time. You can see ..." He coughed again as his gaze flashed up to me. "... by the trouble Aesira has with speaking that it must be true." The faintest tremor laced his words. "Even her horse moves slowly." He motioned to the mare, where she grazed at the speed of a rampaging snail.

The prince flinched. "Is it contagious?"

"No, Prince."

Edwin thrust his shoulders back. With a kick, the hem of his cloak flared again. "Footman, secure that mare."

The driver dismounted. With narrowed eyes, he approached the horse. When he touched the mare's shoulder, he flinched. "Aaaaaaaaaaaaahhhhhhhhhhhhhhhhh." The cry dragged out for nearly a minute as he tried to draw his hand back from the mare.

"Oh. Yes, Prince." Ben winced. "It appears it is contagious."

Great. That will make things so much easier.

Not.

Edwin recoiled, his face a fascinating shade of green. "Driver, stay here with the horse. Don't let anyone touch you." He took a deep breath, trying to regain some composure, I supposed. "Ben." My heart throbbed as Ben glanced up from under his dark lashes. "You'll be driving." The prince climbed into the carriage without another word, slamming the door impressively behind him.

Ben glanced at the carriage and rushed toward me, though he didn't try to touch me. Instead, he held me with his gaze. "Are you all right?"

Heat started toward my cheeks again. "Fine." It sounded like a sigh more than a word.

Ben's brows pressed together. "You'll be better soon enough. Come on. Let's get you home." He motioned for me to follow him to the driver's seat. I did as quickly as able—which was to say, slowly.

Ben stood to the side as I reached up. Up. Up. Inwardly, I winced when my fingers finally landed on the bench. I pushed off the ground with all my strength in the hope to move faster. Instead, I overestimated, and when I finally landed, it was on my face. Dying of embarrassment would have taken too long, so I settled for righting myself, and trying to appear dignified by staring straight ahead, watching from the corners of my eyes as Ben took a seat next to me, though not so close that we would touch if the coach hit a rut. It took him less than a minute to settle himself and pick up the reins, while it had taken me nearly half an hour.

"Don't worry." Ben flicked the reins. The six white horses broke into a swift canter. "Edwin claims he no longer loves Clarissa, but secretly he pines for her. He talks about her in his sleep sometimes—just before I wake him for his morning sword practice. He'll kiss her, and everyone in your kingdom will be restored. Including you."

Not wanting to suffer through the attempt to speak, I nodded. However, that took longer than speaking. I averted my gaze to the fields, trying to focus my thoughts on how the curse apparently only affected living objects. Otherwise, the carriage would be going nowhere fast. I *tried* to think about that, but instead, I ended up thinking about Ben. About how he sat next to me. About how happy that made me. About how it shouldn't have made me happy at all.

"Aesira . . ."

I would have turned to look at him, if I thought I could accomplish that small action before sunset.

The bench creaked as he shifted beside me. I glanced at the one hand that released the reins to rest on the bench next to my fingers—the closest he could get without touching me. Even so, I jerked away—though it seemed more like a breeze brushed my hand into my lap.

I finally looked into his eyes. "You'll get trapped in time." The words crept through the air at the pace of a frenzied sloth, hardly recognizable.

"It would be worth it." His gaze never left mine. "It would be worth it if it meant I could spend the next century with you."

Heat leaked across my cheeks.

Ben had said such things before. All those times Edwin came to court Clarissa, he'd brought Ben with him, and we'd needed to do something while Clarissa and Edwin flirted. So Ben courted me.

However, it was forbidden for servants of different kingdoms to see each other, and when we last spent time together, the cook had found us just as Ben leaned in to kiss me. It would have been my first kiss, if allowed to happen.

Instead, the cook pulled Ben back by his hair and flung him on the ground. With a glower, she leaned over him, a large butcher knife suspended above his neck. She threatened to go to the prince if she ever caught us together again, and if she did, Ben would be executed for his crime.

Because of that, I needed to pretend Ben didn't exist. For his own protection.

Pale lavender tinted the sky by the time we finally reached the castle. Ben drove the carriage right up to the front steps, where he dismounted and approached the carriage door, while I inched toward the edge of the driver's seat.

Just before he touched the handle, Edwin flung it open. "Where is the maiden in distress?"

I jumped off the bench like a feather floating to the ground. When I finally landed, I looked up at the prince. "Room." I was still stuck saying the word when Edwin charged into the castle.

We stared after him for a long moment before Ben turned to me. "I'll walk with you. Lead the way."

I wanted to tell him to leave me alone. To go ahead without me. To keep an eye on prince charming before he lost himself in the castle. However, there wasn't enough time for that. I'd just barely managed to finish saying 'room', after all. Besides, I didn't want him to leave me. Was that a bad thing?

He walked with me. We stepped past other servants also moving in slow motion. Ben easily avoided them, though my heart jumped every time just the same. I didn't want him to be caught in Clarissa's horrid curse, nor to suffer a century of staring at the same piece of wall.

The sun kissed the horizon by the time we reached the princess's room. Someone had laid Clarissa on her bed, and they'd even tucked a ruby red rose between her clasped hands.

Edwin paced next to her, glancing toward Clarissa and away again every other moment.

"What's happened? Didn't you kiss her?" I wanted to ask but gave up when I realized the words wouldn't come in any reasonable time frame.

"Why haven't you kissed the princess?" Ben asked him. "The whole kingdom is waiting for you!"

"I did!" Edwin continued to pace, moving faster than my eyes could follow. "Several times! I've kissed her, proclaimed my undying love for her, and even sang her a ballad! Nothing's happened!"

My heart dropped as my knees gave way. I sank towards the floor.

"But the curse!" Ben pushed hair from his eyes. "The witch said the only way to save the kingdom was by true love's kiss!"

Edwin spun around, flinging his arms out like an octopus. "I know. I know! And I've tried, but nothing's happened. Watch!" He turned back and leaned over his sleeping beauty. Roughly, he kissed her lips. In her sleep, Clarissa smiled, yet made no motion to wake.

I continued to sink to the floor. Even though my body moved

slowly, my mind raced. Did I forget something? Remember the story wrong? It *was* true love's kiss that would work.

Right?

I winced. *No!* "First ..."

Ben turned to me.

One tear leaked out of my eye, crawling down my cheek. "Kiss ..."

A little round circle of comprehension formed on Ben's lips.

"What's she saying now?" Edwin asked from across the room.

Ben turned to Edwin. "*First* kiss." He smacked his own forehead. "How did I forget? It's true love's *first* kiss that's supposed to break the spell."

Edwin leaned over Clarissa. His hands tightened on hers. Voice shaking, he said, "Well this definitely isn't our first kiss. We've been dating on and off for over a year. I can't take all those kisses back." His voice cracked on the last word.

My thoughts echoed Ben's words. How did I forget? My mistake would cost us the entire kingdom. It would cost me my life.

It would cost me Ben.

As my knees finally touched the floor, my gaze slid upward. Tears struggled to escape, pooling in the corners of my eyes, brimming over my lashes but not yet falling.

Ben's lips pressed into a thin line as his brows pushed together. His eyes glistened, too, though tears did not escape. Not like mine, which slithered down my cheeks. It was just like the last time we'd met—when we'd almost kissed. When we'd said goodbye and he'd wiped the tear from my face.

He reached for me as if to catch my tears again.

My heart breaking, I turned my head away. I couldn't let him touch me. "Go." The word slid into the air like a breath.

I meant the word for Ben alone, yet Edwin, leaning over Clarissa, said, "There's nothing we can do, Ben." The prince moved as though he'd been infected with the curse too, but by how fast he blinked his tears away, I knew he hadn't actually been captured by time. "Let's go." Edwin turned, tucking his chin as he ducked through the door.

Ben hung back. "Aesira …" He stared at me, his hand still outstretched, about to touch me. To hold me. To wipe away my tears. "I don't know what to say."

I did.

Taking a shallow breath, I forced my gaze back up to his. As darkness fell around us, I opened my mouth. "Ben … I …" Even as I formed the words, and screamed them inside my head, my lips froze. I froze. Completely. Unalterably.

I'd kneel for the next century, staring up at where Ben once stood, my declaration frozen on my lips.

Ben, I love you …

He'd never hear the words. He'd die before the curse released me.

Ben turned his back to me. His shoulders shook. My heart broke, too. I wished to close my eyes. I wished to turn away. Better yet, I wished to fling myself into his arms to tell him everything would be all right.

Instead, I knelt there. Trapped. Watching him weep as my frozen heart yearned to beat for him. Him alone. Him forever and ever.

For a long time Ben lingered, pacing through the beams of moonlight spilling in through the window. Every time his gaze strayed to me, he broke into tears.

Go, I wanted to say. *Edwin's waiting for you. Go, I'll be all right.*

As if he heard my thoughts, Ben finally turned to the door.

He didn't look at me again. His boots rang on the marble as he strode out of my line of sight.

Silence sank around me, broken only by Clarissa's even breathing as she slept—oblivious to the chaos she'd created, to the hearts she'd broken, and the lives she'd shattered.

My thoughts turned to Ben again. How could they not? There was no reason for me to stop myself. He wouldn't be killed for loving me. I'd never see him again in my lifetime, so what did it matter whether or not I loved him?

I do, I admitted to myself. *I do love him.*

"Aesira." His voice startled me from my thoughts.

Ben!

A burst of longing spread through my frozen body, as he emerged through the door, walking slowly, deliberately. He knelt across from me so close our knees almost touched.

He gazed down into my eyes. I wondered if he knew I could hear him. "I meant what I said. I would rather be frozen in time with you for a hundred years—or even a thousand—or even a million—if it meant I could be with you, my sleepless beauty."

He leaned forward, his lips brushing mine as soft and gentle as a rose petal before firming with his sincerity. As warmth spread through me, chasing away the chill that froze my heart, I wished I could kiss him back.

My lips softened to match the shape of his.

I jumped as I opened my eyes; when had they closed? Jerking away from Ben, I dragged in a breath of air, so quick it stunned me.

What is going on?

Ben leaned back and laughed as he pulled me to my feet. With one hand, he pushed his hair out of his eyes, blinking hard as if he couldn't believe what he saw.

"What happened?" I asked—quickly, crisply.

"I don't care!" He pulled me close and kissed me again.

"What is going on?" Clarissa sat up on her bed.

We jumped apart. Though she'd been asleep all day, not a golden hair stood out of place on Clarissa's head. She flung the rose away with a snort of disgust as she stood, her glossy skirts shimmering in the starlight. "Aesira, what are you doing? Who's that?" She glanced around her lavish bedroom. "Where's Edwin?"

"I, uh ..." My heart froze, so I couldn't speak as I remembered what would happen if Ben and I were caught together "I ... just ... well ..."

"Edwin is gone, Princess." Ben took my hand. "He left when he couldn't wake you."

Clarissa stared at us—her face stiffened in a perfect mask of shock. For a moment, I wondered if the curse had jumped back into affect.

"He—" Her jaw worked furiously. "What do you—of course he—what do you mean he couldn't *wake* me? His kiss should have ended all of this! Like the witch said! *Our* kiss should have saved *everyone*! Shown everyone the strength of our love!"

I was confused, too.

"True love's *first* kiss," Ben said. "You and Edwin aren't exactly ... er ... so, well ... I think we ..." He squeezed my fingers.

I spun to face him. "*Our* first kiss broke the spell?"

"*What?*" Clarissa's tiny hands clenched into fists while her eye twitched. "Do you two ... love each other?"

It would be treason to answer that question in the affirmative. Yet, as I thought back on everything Ben had said, and about what I had realized as I sat frozen—fearing I'd never see Ben again—I knew only one answer could be given. "Yes," I said. "And I'd rather die than live without him."

I almost expected her to fulfill the terms of my statement, and not in the happily ever after sort of way, when Edwin burst into the room.

"The servants all woke up so I thought!" His gaze landed on the princess, whose frown vanished, replaced with an insipid smile and cheeks as pink as her dress. "My love!" He rushed to her and picked her up, spinning her around. She yelped, and the moment he set her down, he kissed her.

It didn't seem wise to point out how, only hours earlier, Edwin swore to never ever, *ever* get back together with Clarissa.

"Are you ..." I cleared my throat, not sure if Clarissa heard me over the sound of, well, smacking lips. "Are you going to punish us?" The question needed to be answered.

As she came up for air, her lips pursed, or maybe they were stuck that way from kissing.

The silence stretched out too long. Edwin glanced from Ben to me. He cocked one eyebrow. "Are you two ..."

"Yes," Ben said without hesitation.

Edwin spun to Clarissa, who entwined her arm with his as she tapped one finger to her chin. "We won't punish you ..." Clarissa said, "If ..." She placed her palm on Edwin's chest.

It took me a moment to realize Ben supported most of my weight. My legs shook too much to hold me.

Edwin straightened. "If you never ever, *ever* tell *anyone* that *your* kiss broke the spell, and not *ours*."

Something so simple? I stifled a laugh as Ben stepped forward and gave a small bow. "As you wish."

Clarissa sighed. "Well, that's that then. Now go find your happily ever after in some other room, or something."

After the door closed behind us, Ben laughed. One arm wrapped around my waist as we trailed down a stairwell.

Though night slept thick around us, people crowded the

castle, celebrating. I pulled Ben into a niche housing a suit of armor. He hugged me close, and as he rested his chin in my hair, I said, "I can't believe they let us off so easy! It's not as if anyone will ever remember the events of tonight, anyway. Even if they do, I'd give up all the fame and glory to be with you."

"Who can say why they did it?" His breath rippled through my hair like a warm breeze, reminding me of our sunlight-like kiss.

I pressed my head into his chest. "I love you."

He gave a laugh like a soft sigh. "You don't need to whisper it. We're in the clear. We can shout to the world we're together."

"Forever?"

"Yes." He kissed the top of my head. "For ever and ever and ever."

Acknowledgements

For Tyler.

My gratitude to Sarah Durtschi, Miranda McNeff, Mariah McNeff, Ashley Gephart, and Ashlee Johnson: the network of writers who helped me chisel out what I was trying to say in this piece before I could embarrass myself with typos in front of publishers. Well, more typos.

Special thanks to Jen Heikkila of "Simply Sublime Photography" for the wonderful author photo she took of me. Man, I look good!

A unique thanks to Ross Hanson for letting me borrow his computer—without which, I would have missed the deadline for the anthology submissions. Hooray for midnight submissions!

And of course, the highest gratitude to my parents, Alan and Nolana, who taught me to always follow my dreams. And to read books. Lots of books.

Kimberly Kay

When Kimberly was younger, she was incredibly timid. She didn't talk much because she was afraid of what others would think of her. Instead, she expressed herself through drawing. Eventually, art alone wasn't enough. There were some things she couldn't express with pencils, so she began talking, and when she did, she realized she had something to say. Now no one can get her to shut up! Worse, she's discovered she can put those words into writing to share what she has to say with even more people. Kimberly writes short stories and novels—usually fantasy fairytale retellings. Scattered within her works are things she loves: horses, fencing, archery, and so much more. With her friends, she writes fun fan-fiction that expands her creativity, (and shows what a nerd she is). Through writing, she has found confidence and freedom.

Stage Fright

Erika Beebe

J. Taylor Publishing

They warned me about the stage.

It stretched out long, black and ice-hard with a curve around the edge, and Mean Girl, one of the cast members, stood at the perfect angle, a little behind me off to the left, exactly where I couldn't escape her sneer. *"Do you remember the last time you danced on the lake, right before the blizzard in the spring?"* my best friend Jess had asked the night before, in a long overdue FaceTime chat—the closest we'd come to seeing each other in months. *"Feel the ice, and dance."*

I sucked in a huge breath of air and pictured that day in my hometown, instead of the stage; the sky overhead had darkened, the rolling clouds pushed by a wind so strong it whipped my long dark hair around my face. I remembered braiding my hair quickly and pulling my green stocking hat down over my ears and forehead. After grabbing my skates, I'd slung them over my shoulder and walked to the edge of the frozen lake.

I can do this.

Wearing my nude-colored heels and trying not to fall, I stepped forward over the stage's smooth surface, stronger, calmer. I'd never worn heels before. I'd also never scored the lead role in a school musical.

"Oh, just kiss him," the stage cast sang out to me.

Dressed in their Shakespearean best, the girls twirled across the stage in their flowy dresses, while the boys strutted around in their tight black pants and tall boots. A cardboard painted town stretched from one end of the curtain to the other as Sam, my leading man, cast as Petruchio, pursued me, grabbing my hand and trying to hang on.

I slid out of his grasp and ran from his arms, playing his new wife in the musical *Kiss Me, Kate*, who didn't want a man, and definitely didn't want to kiss him to seal the deal at the end of act one.

I didn't want to kiss the boys on the ice either. Not when I'd known them my whole life. Their secrets—their gangly growth spurts—every pimple and hair and awkward bodily sound.

"You're lucky I didn't hit you!"

"You're lucky I didn't knock you on your butts!" I'd said back.

"With what? Your awesome swing of your hips, because, Hannah, I can think of a lot more useful things we can do than skate," Eddie, the tallest one, had said.

I'd crossed my arms over my chest and shifted back, tilting my head. *"Really? Because, from what I just saw, if that's how you handle a stick, why would I believe you could handle a kiss?"*

I didn't need a small town boy to make me feel good. I wanted a life beyond my farm. I wanted a boy to travel the world with me.

I'd launched myself off the frozen dirt and onto the ice, pushing against the skates, my thighs screaming in protest as I forced the blood through my muscles so I could push faster.

Jess was right. On the ice, I danced free. I stepped firm on the stage, pressing through my calves and straight to my heels.

I will survive these shoes. I will own this stage.

Inhaling, I expanded my chest, fighting against the tightness of the dress. My costume, a wedding dress made of white satin, didn't fit me. Too tight in the bust, too loose in the shoulders, it went way longer than it should have to justify the ridiculous heels our drama teacher, Mr. Jerome, swore I had to wear.

My right sleeve fell loose down my shoulder, bubbling low like a lump out of place. I glanced down, wanting to pull up the sleeve, but not about to risk drawing attention to the dress and adding another worry to my plate. I needed to get through the practice performance built of my classmates, my teachers, and all the people I needed to prove wrong. I was no invisible small town girl, and if I could make my feet work in the heels, like I'd always made the skates work on the ice back home, they would have to see me for real, and maybe even look at me with a little respect.

The stage cast gathered like a fence in front of me, blocking my escape from Sam. Mean Girl threw her arms in the air, sending me backwards a few steps like we rehearsed. Her gaze fell toward the sleeve hanging limp on my arm, and a wicked smile curled up her lips. The cast surrounded her instead of me, staying close in a circle while avoiding one of Mr. Jerome's warning glares, something he did a lot during the week of practice. Mr. Jerome reminded me of my Dad with his big dimples, his warm smile, the balding head he should have shaved but didn't, and his determination. He'd threatened everyone in class with a failing grade if they didn't act as they should. I should have been used to their defiance; I'd even confessed to Jess how taking Kate's part had been good for boosting my horrible mood, but bad for my social life, earning me a second death sentence in a school where one was bad enough.

"*Then, what else do you have to lose, Hannah? Blow them away,*" Jess's voice blew through my head.

I grabbed the left sleeve on the dress and yanked it off my other shoulder, smiling sweetly back at Mean Girl. She stopped grinning, lips freezing into a straight line mid-stanza, but she never fell silent.

The only other time she went blank like that was the moment everyone knew *I* scored the lead role in the play, and Mean Girl became my understudy. Our drama class had gathered in front Mr. Jerome's office door, where he always taped up the news. I'd walked up late—at the very back of the crowd. Eyes turned my way, and the silence hung so thick in the air I couldn't breathe.

Knuckles cracked. A whisper leaked out.

"That little thief!" Mean Girl had shattered the silence.

The crowd parted. She ripped the paper off the door, spun around on her heels and marched up to me, shoving the paper in *my* face. "First my boyfriend. Now the play. I don't know what planet you came from. I don't care who you know. Ever since you moved here, you've been trying to steal my life. You're going to burn for this, Hannah."

A couple of boys in the crowd *oooohed.*

"Wait!" I'd yelled, needing a second to think. I grabbed my head, spinning around to catch her gaze, but she tore off down the hall, stomping up a storm of anger. "I didn't want the part! I didn't mean to hurt you! You can have it!"

She didn't stop, and the crowd followed, just like always.

On stage, the cast eyed me with overly exaggerated smiles, singing out, "Oh, just kiss him!"

I jerked my head at Sam and stepped backwards, warning him to stay put with my glare.

"Kiss me!" He projected his voice above their chanting just like Mr. Jerome had showed us, booming over us with authority and telling us it came from our gut.

We danced down the stage with a foot of space between our bodies, him moving at me, and me matching his steps backwards, steering clear of his trap to steal a kiss. The cast parted in two rows around us, and Mean Girl twirled loose from the line, her bright yellow dress whirling around her, her eyes throwing a dagger's glare at me over Sam's shoulder. She spun off again, passing behind my back.

I swallowed, slightly panicked, when I couldn't see her.

Hands touched my back.

"Don't trip," Mean Girl mumbled near my ear, distracting me as she shoved me straight into Sam.

He caught me as I slipped on the stage, and he moved quickly into his next action with the rope, lassoing me and helping me recover, which I did, remembering to spin away just barely out of his reach.

So brave, I thought at Mean Girl, and glanced at Mr. Jerome hiding behind the curtain, clutching the playbook to his chest with his face exploding beet red. He had to know. I hoped he'd yank her off stage at the end of the scene and tell her to knock it off. He'd helped me out all week with her, growling under his breath, *"Keep it up, Liz, and you'll lose your understudy status."*

The pressure of the rope tightened around my waist, and I circled into Sam, so close to his body the ruffles in his white Shakespeare-style shirt swallowed some of my dress. Funny how the dress probably fit Mean Girl perfectly; her mom had been commissioned to make it after all.

"Just kiss me, Kate," Sam sang to me, reminding me I should be playing tug-a-war with him.

I leaned my face away and pushed him back with my hands, just like Mr. Jerome coached me to, "No!"

I struggled; Sam yanked me back, and we danced the fight until the rope fell off, and I rushed to the front of the stage with the edges of my dress swishing like water against my legs. A strand of my long dark hair snuck loose from under the sparkly tiara fastened tightly to my head. I ignored the hair and the pain from the pins pressing down on my scalp. Actresses never wore pain or annoyance on their faces; they acted above it.

Looking at my feet—a terrible mistake—I bobbled on my heels. *Steady,* I thought, wishing my ankles strong. Mr. Jerome warned us—me actually, since everyone else seemed to know how to maneuver in heels—to never look at my feet. *"You're gone if you do,"* he'd said. I never looked at my skates on the ice, but all of a sudden I couldn't picture the ice anymore, scared my legs would betray me.

I tried to imagine the ice under my feet again, seeing myself in skates instead of heels. The stage floor wouldn't give; it didn't help me get my balance back the way the ice could. My heart started to pound. My cheeks warmed.

"Your dad would want you to have the lead," Mr. Jerome had said to me after I'd stormed into his office demanding an explanation when I hadn't even tried out for the part.

"How do you know?" I had asked with the tears burning up my eyes.

"We grew up together, and he told me he wanted you to get out of that small town. He told me he wanted you to make a name for yourself and you'd never have a chance back home."

Home wasn't black and covered with lights, and while Mr. Jerome might have believed I made a great Kate, faced with the stage and the ridiculous heels, I needed the ice, and it was slipping away.

The trill of the bird made me whirl around to gaze at the painted backdrop of trees and hills, as if searching it out. I returned its song, singing back, letting acted hope widen my eyes. One of the chorus men stepped between the bird and me. When it called again, I echoed back, and we played that game until a fake gun fired off and, backstage, a ball hit the floor.

A white glove lay still in the middle of the stage—my imaginary bird, dead.

Shocked and upset, I stretched my arm toward the bird, mimicking the action I'd seen in the original nineteen-fifties movie of our play. I'd watched it over and over again to get every movement and gesture just right. I'd said my lines so many times I thought I dreamed Kate's dreams more than my own.

"Kiss me, Kate," Sam said, grabbing my hand.

I spun into his chest, into the spotlight and gave him my best squinty eyes even as the fake lashes stuck to my eyelids. I couldn't help thinking maybe I should have let Mean Girl have the part.

"Dastard," I called him, slipping away to the front of the stage, hoping I appeared graceful to the audience.

The lights glared down so bright a sheen of sweat broke across my face. Sam said something from behind me, but I didn't understand, concentrating on my balance, concentrating on not falling.

He grabbed my hand. "I've got you."

"For now," I whispered, knowing Sam held on for the show, and only the show. He was one of Mean Girl's friends, after all.

Bright spotlights fought through the endless sea of black beyond the stage. Their harsh fingers heated my skin as I faced the first row in the crowd. I barely recognized anyone with the light and the black wrestling in the air. *Chiaro—Chiaroscuro*, is what Mr. Jerome called it, a fancy Italian word for contrast. A blessing, too, covering most of the faces in a thick dark blanket so I couldn't see the reactions from my high school classmates—whether they wore respect, or not.

Caught at a dangerous angle, my ankles trying to fold and Sam hanging on, I blinked a few times. The haze cleared from my vision, a face in the crowd with strong lines outlined in a shimmery halo of light took form.

"Hannah, you're not alone."

Huh? That wasn't Sam. It came from the halo. I touched my head and blinked. Sam's arm tugged me, but I stepped backwards, moving to the end of the stage and staring straight ahead.

The cast on stage chimed, "Kiss him," over and over, grabbing me and passing me down the line of hands to Sam, who wrestled me into a dip.

"Kiss me," Sam said leaning over me, ordering me stronger than we'd practiced, and holding on to me so tight his fingers dug through the dress pinching my skin.

I should have said something, or rather sung something. Instead, I pushed Sam back as he pulled me forward, and a glimmer of worry flashed in his eyes.

Sweat dripped down my back. Sam tilted his chin down. "Sing," he whispered in my ear.

I didn't know the pitch. I couldn't think of the first word.

Cast members filled the empty air with a continued chorus of, "Kiss him," and smiling a little too big.

"Come on, Hannah," Sam said, his lips not moving. "Sing!"

My gaze danced all over his face. My heart thumped in my chest, racing in my ears. I couldn't remember anything with that strange halo still burning in my mind and clouding my vision.

I closed my eyes, dizzy, my heart thudding so loud I couldn't hear anything else. I shut out the noise on the stage, breathing and trying to get control—until I realized the singing had stopped, and the world fell silent.

My lids flew open, thinking Mean Girl got her way, and the whole cast had all risked their grade just to embarrass me. Sam, like all the others, refused to make Mean Girl mad, most of the time.

He just stared down at my face with large frozen—serious—eyes.

"Sam?" I whispered.

He didn't move. He didn't blink. I touched his face; nothing happened. He still held on to me, but his fingers were ice cold. I didn't like cold things even though I liked to skate; I hated the snow and the winter air that always snuck in through every hole, stealing my breath, and covering all the streets so high that driving was next to impossible. On the ice, though, I was warm and free.

On stage, I yanked my hand away and glanced slowly over my shoulder at the cast. No one moved, their bodies' statue-still just like Sam.

I turned my head to the front, my own breath crashing in my chest. The bows in the orchestra pit hung frozen in the air. The audience, everyone, waited, watching me, unmoving like Sam and the stage cast—except for a boy walking slowly down the center aisle of the theater.

I wiggled loose from Sam and tumbled to the floor. *This isn't real.*

"You'll choke under the spotlight. You're not strong enough to fight the lights," Mean Girl had said in front of everyone, just as the curtain lifted before the show. Of course the whole class had to chime in with, *"The lights will get you Hannah. They get everyone on this stage the first time."*

I couldn't choke. *It's stage fright. Get over it, Hannah. Get off the floor.* I didn't think I could handle an ounce more of public humiliation. I stood up carefully and glanced toward the crowd in the dark. The boy moved faster down the center aisle, glowing under the spotlight. He cut to the side, climbed the steps to the top of the stage, and stopped in front of the principal, who stood against the far wall with crossed arms and a tilted chin.

The boy slapped the principal on the cheek three quick times, and my mouth fell open. No one treated the principal like that.

"Not invincible like you thought, huh?" His voice echoed from across the stage.

I couldn't tell if he said it to the principal, or me.

Nothing made sense—not the frozen crowd, the eerie silence in the theater, or the strange boy walking across the stage with soundless feet. *Should I run?*

Before I could answer myself, he stood in my personal space—so close my own chest locked up for a moment, leaving me afraid I might freeze up, too.

I studied his face—his gorgeous straight lines, tan skin, and eyes bleeding blue like the sky, sparkly with light. Hair the color of a moonless night stuck up all wild around his head. Some part of me thought I knew him. He looked so familiar, the way a song sometimes sounds, even when I've never heard it before.

The boy took my hand. "Now, this is how you do it," he said with a voice smooth like air, kissing the back of my hand.

In that moment, nothing else mattered. His dreamy mouth with full lips and a tiny knowing smile drew me in. He leaned closer, his gaze stuck on my lips, his lips lingering millimeters above me.

"This is your show, Hannah." His breath reached my mouth, and I couldn't tell if the air moving between my lips was his or mine. "You can move. You can do whatever you want, and they won't stop you. I made sure of that."

How could he? What sort of person could do that? *You're freaking out. This isn't real.* "Who are you?" I whispered, trying to quiet the million thoughts flying through my head.

"You don't recognize me?"

I searched my mind—his nose, mouth, eyebrows. I wanted to say 'yes!', but I couldn't lie. I started to open my mouth to say something, but he silenced me when he folded one of my hands against his chest, giving me a connection to his heart—beating, real—and his hands warmed my body.

"You made me," he said, still holding my hand and guiding my fingers to his lips. "These," he said, speaking against my fingertips. "The picture above your desk. At the very top of the others, and this ..." He traced one of my fingers over the slope of his nose. "... That one still lies free on top of your desk. The magazine you tore it from is already rolled up in the trash."

The magazine. All my magazines. Most nights, I sat on my bed with *Teen Vogue* on my lap, passing my fingers over the slick pages, imagining what it would be like to be in pictures with the guys. Famous people worked hard, learning music, writing songs, performing, trying. Sweating to make their dreams come true. So talented—not the boys I grew up with, and definitely not like the boys in Minneapolis, getting all sorts of handouts just like Mr. Jerome had said. *"This performance could earn the scholarship you need to have anything you want, Hannah. Don't let them define you. You graduate in two months. They'll be here, getting handouts from their parents and cursing you because you made something of yourself, all on your own."*

I stared at the floor and breathed slow through my mouth, trying to bring the calm back into my head. My hands went to Gorgeous boy's hair.

He hung on to my fingers and traced them down to his cheek resting them on his chin. "The hair, the skin, it's all from the same photo in the center. The largest one. The one you kept gazing at this morning right before you left for school. Remember? It made you late. Your mom had to call you twice."

I remembered. That morning had been harder than most

days. I didn't want to get out of bed. I'd stayed up too late talking with Jess, when I confessed I thought playing Kate had been a good decision, when she'd told me to think about our hometown lake whenever I got nervous, and after we talked about the heels and the ice, I asked her if she got the magazine I sent her. She had. We'd flipped through together, me much slower than her.

The edges of the pages in the same magazine had folded around my knees, and I'd stared at his giant face in the centerfold—black hair, tan skin; he melted my heart.

"Do you see him?" I'd asked Jess.

"Yeah. I see the pain in his eyes, too. Who wants a boy with baggage?"

"Gotta go, Jess."

"You're going to add that to your picture collage, aren't you? That's not right, Hannah. Those boys won't ever be real. I want someone real. To feel their hot lips, and do you remember—"

"I don't care." I cut her off. *"I love him."* I'd hung up the phone, ripped out the picture from the magazine, walked to my desk, and cut off all the rough edges around the page, smoothing the picture down on my desk with my hands. The pain in his eyes meant he'd understand me. He, that photo, had made me late, with Mom threatening to tear them all up if I didn't hurry. She always knew where to jab me—her gift with the verbal knife.

"It's okay, Hannah." Gorgeous boy's hands touched my face. "I'm here now, and you were right. We do get each other."

"Wait," I said, my lip shaking, mind trying to grab what everything meant.

"You have nothing to be afraid of, anymore," he said, brushing my face with his fingers. "And now, Hannah, if you ask me to kiss you, I'm yours—forever—and they'll never hurt you again."

He leaned closer, his eyes drinking me in. My belly warmed. Heat spread through me, and I wanted him to kiss me. I pulled my hands away from his chest and wrapped them around his neck. His arms slid around me, pulling me closer.

"What's your name?" It seemed suddenly important.

"Gabriel."

The password to my laptop on my desk. The perfect name. The name from church I heard the last time I went with my Dad—before he never returned from the war in Iraq. He'd left us alone on a farm, with cows and a tractor and a folded flag my mother couldn't bear to look at. I'd yelled at him when I found out he volunteered to go, and with mom falling apart and refusing to take me, I hadn't gone to church since then. Yet, Gabriel stood in front of me.

"If I ask you to kiss me, what—what will happen, exactly?" I stumbled over the lump in my throat, his silky hair sliding between my fingers.

"I'll take you away from here. You said you wanted to travel the world, right?"

I had said that. I'd said it to the computer screen in the dark in the middle of the night, most nights, typing away on my laptop when I couldn't sleep, eaten alive inside with loneliness. Not even my mom knew about my dreams. I never shared them because she cried all the time, so I kept my tears locked up for just me, in my room, and nobody seemed to want me.

Gabriel did, and my mind raced with wanting. I wanted to kiss him. I wanted him to take me away, to show me all the places in my history book; the palazzos in Italy, the Eiffel tower in France. Pyramids, mountains, the promise of anything and everything danced in his eyes.

"Say it." His voice made me shiver. He pulled me close to

him again, his hand hot against my face while his other arm still wrapped around me.

I'd never been kissed. I'd never been on a date in my whole life.

"You can have everything you ever dreamed, just ask me to kiss you."

Kiss me, I thought. The play. Sam. I glanced over at his frozen figure, wondering. If Gabriel kissed me, would anyone remember I ever existed? Would I just disappear with him? My mom had no one else but me. She'd cry—if she had any tears left.

Gabriel gestured behind his back.

The stage lights dimmed. My world disappeared, absorbed in all the darkness. The curtain whooshed out from the walls, sweeping the stage and cutting me off from the crowd in front.

Sucked up in the black world, I knew what to sing. *"No,"* appeared out of nowhere, drifting through my thoughts. The one line I'd forgotten. The one I couldn't help but say even as Gabriel held on tight, and Sam stayed frozen, and Mean Girl went on being mean.

"No."

I opened my eyes. Sam leaned over me lit up in all the lights again, and I blinked, confused. No Gabriel. No closed curtains. I was back in Sam's arms like I'd never left. The audience out front moved and wiggled around in their seats, waiting for the end of the first act.

Sam straightened, taking me with him, while the cast sang their hearts out behind us on the stage, dancing and shuffling between each other. His arm came around me, firm like we rehearsed. I beat against his chest with more force than I should have.

I spun around toward the crowd but couldn't find any trace

of Gabriel. I didn't want Sam. I didn't want life on the stage. I wanted Gabriel to come back and hold me again. Why didn't I ask him to kiss me? *Because you've gone nuts and he wasn't real.* I wanted to leave and never come back.

Sam held me so tight it almost hurt.

"What's gotten into you?" he asked.

I winced and looked up at his face. He should have thrown me over his shoulder right then. We should have left the stage together with me kicking and screaming and a quick spanking on my back side as punishment for running away. All he wanted was a kiss. I refused, being the shrew in the town with no one left to marry me but Sam's character—the whole point of that part of the play.

Instead, something sparkled in his eyes. Those strange star-filled eyes. "I won't let go," Sam said to me, but it wasn't his voice; Gabriel spoke through his lips.

I yanked myself away from him, just as the lights snuffed out and the blackness stole the life from the stage. It stole me right out of Sam's arms, too.

"What happened?" Mr. Jerome stomped towards us full of fury.

"I don't know," Sam said, scratching his head and seeming himself once more.

"You've rehearsed it all week. You've been perfect. No excuses, Sam and Hannah," Mr Jerome said, but I was too far gone to listen to anything he might say.

Gabriel. The boy. The dream. It couldn't be real. I imagined the whole thing. Tears started to fall.

"Are you okay?" Sam asked.

"No," I whispered. I clenched my hands, defeated, hurt, disappointed and hit with a sudden surge of anger. My face burned with it. Anger at Mean Girl. Anger at myself for looking like a fool in front of everyone. Anger at Sam for not being Gabriel on the stage when I came out of my vision.

Mean Girl approached, smiling all smug and proud. "I told you, Mr. Jerome. I told you she'd crack."

I did. I yanked off the tiara and pulled every one of the pins loose from my hair, throwing them on the floor. My hair sprung out, falling around my shoulders in long rings of curls from being pulled back and tied up so close to my head.

"You," I said, stepping in to face off with Mean Girl. Her smile fell off her face and she took a step back as I bore into her eyes with mine. "I tried everything, all year, to get you to like me." I knew the types of clothes she wore and used most of my savings from my part-time job at the coffee shop in town to make sure I bought the same things: the Miss Me Jeans, the Boutique tops, the scarves and the boots, because if I couldn't beat them, I'd try to join them. I'd suffered every day.

I grabbed her wrist, turned up her hand, and slapped the tiara in it so hard I hoped it stung. My Dad had always said, *"Make friends, Hannah, they get you through life."* He didn't know Mean Girl. "You win. It's not worth the fight, and I don't need it to be happy. I don't want anything that has to do with you anymore."

Mean Girl crossed her arms as the tears rolled down my hot cheeks. I sniffed, rubbing my eyes gently with my fingers, and watched her place the tiara carefully on her head. "About time you learned your rank. You'll always be second, Hannah," she said with a grin built of victory.

Our teacher stepped up behind me. "Liz, give Hannah the tiara back, and Hannah, don't do this. You earned the part."

I pulled off the stupid heels, one at a time, and cast them to the side of the stage. Mean Girl didn't budge, the tiara still sparkling on her head.

"What are you doing?" Mr. Jerome asked. "What about your Dad?"

I looked up at the mention of my Dad. Mr. Jerome and my Dad had grown up together, but Mr. Jerome left town on a mission to *act,* and my Dad stayed behind, marrying my mom right out of high school. "I've never met people who could have anything they wanted, but what they want the most is to hurt me. Do you have any idea what it feels like to try so hard and fail every day?"

"I do." He'd once convinced me that keeping the lead role would make my life change, that I'd do so well in the play everyone around me would see I was worth something, deserved respect, and would start to like me.

It had only gotten worse. "Good. Then you see that no one wins here. Not you. Not my mom. Not my dad." Even at eighteen, I knew I needed to make my biggest dream happen—to move away from all of the cold and go somewhere new.

He shut his mouth and stepped to the side.

I shot off the stage, wrestling through the edge of the velvety black curtain. I found a hole and ran straight out the back door, down the hall, the white gown rippling around my legs. I kept going to the dressing room, grabbed my coat and my black furry boots, and burst through the exit at the end of the hall, a blast of cold air hitting me like a frozen sheet of ice.

"Hannah."

God, I am going crazy. I couldn't shake Gabriel's voice.

Snow covered the grass around the edges of the school, like it had since early fall. Before, we had to borrow someone's four-wheel-drive vehicle with chains on the tires every week. I couldn't just go to a mall or even a movie theater, not with the snow everywhere; it took a good three hours to drive the hundred and twenty miles to a decent town. I'd prayed every day back then to get out of the small world and into the big. No one ever told me, though, that I might not want my prayers answered.

I wrapped my coat around me, tighter than Gabriel's arms had been. *I'm such an idiot. Jess was right. I can't even fall for a real guy. I imagine them.*

Running through the middle of the parking lot, I weaved through aisles of packed cars, not remembering where I'd parked. My toes burned with the cold, my fingers had gone numb. Even as I wrapped my arms around myself and gazed over the snow-covered vehicles, I couldn't find it.

"You look a little lost," a guy's voice shot out at me. I turned around slow, hoping for a miracle and knowing the one I wanted would never come true.

"No more than you," I said, studying the stranger.

"Good point." Slumped against a midnight blue Jeep Wrangler, the kind the boys drove back home with the circle lights and giant off-road tires, he stood tall in his brown, furry coat.

"Nice Jeep," I said, moving a loose strand of my hair out of my eyes.

He pulled off his hood and tucked his gloved hands in his pockets. "Thanks. My Dad just bought it. He felt bad for me, I guess, dragging me from California, all the way here to blizzardville."

"That explains the tan, then, huh?" I said, taking a step toward him.

He gave me a killer smile. His eyes dark, hair dark—I couldn't keep myself from tilting my head just a little; he reminded me of someone.

"I'm Ben, by the way."

"Hannah."

Ben's face tilted down, and I followed his gaze to the dress poking out underneath my waist-length coat. "Is that ... are you wearing a wedding dress?"

I cursed myself for not changing out of the stupid dress, but smiled because Mean Girl didn't have it. "Yeah." I chuckled. "I was supposed to be in a play today."

"Supposed to, eh?" Ben asked. "What'd you do, leave him at the altar? Let me guess." He tilted his chin. "He was secretly cheating on you with the meanest girl in the school."

"Something like that."

Snow swirled around the top of his Jeep in a burst of cold wind. It stuck to my face and in my lashes; I blinked it away.

Ben rubbed his arms. "I'm freezing, and your teeth are chattering. You want to get out of here and go somewhere warm?"

I kicked his tire with my boot. A pile of snow fell on the top of the toe, and I shook it off. I hated being alone. I hated fighting people every day just to prove I was a real person. Dad wouldn't fault me if those people in the play didn't want to be my friend, especially if someone else did, right? "Somewhere warm sounds like the best plan ever."

Ben opened the door and signaled me in with a cute grin and an exaggerated bow.

"No one's been this nice to me in months," I said, grinning just a little and turning around to face him. I caught his gaze searching mine.

"You're not from here, are you?" he asked. "Because the girls around here don't look you in the eyes. Not straight on like you."

"No. I'm a small town girl. My Dad taught me to look people in the eye. You can see what they're made of that way."

Ben leaned in close, his hand still holding the door open. "He sounds like a good man."

"Was." I looked down and back up immediately.

"Sorry to hear that. I would have liked to have met him."

I wish he was still here. When Dad left for the war last year, I'd never told him I loved him—my gut too proud to cave at being left alone with mom in a snowstorm with diagonal white sheets falling from the sky.

I slid down in the seat. Paper crinkled underneath me. Shifting to the side, I withdrew a magazine stuck under my coat. My smile fell when my gaze landed on the boy on the cover. I flipped to the center, to the two-page spread. It was him. The picture I couldn't stop staring at that morning, the one that made me late for school—the magazine I'd thrown in the trash, right before my mom had threatened to tear off all of the pictures on my wall for making her late. I touched the familiar glossy paper.

The driver side door opened and Ben sat inside, shutting out the cold but not bringing the warmth back. "You look like you've seen a ghost."

I glanced over at him. His dark eyes sparkled with a glimmer of blue—Gabriel's blue. His smile, his lips, his nose—was Ben really Ben?

He glanced toward the magazine in my lap. "Oh, that's my sister's. She likes to look at pictures of all the hot guys."

I didn't know what to say.

Ben fired up the engine. "So, where to, because you know, I am the 'new guy'." He quoted the air with his fingers.

"You came back," I said out of nowhere and covered my mouth. "I'm sorry—"

"You okay?"

I glanced at my lap and realized my dress had snuck up a little high on my leg; I swiped it back down.

Ben coughed into his fist. "I know of place with a really

warm fire and—"

"Ben?" I broke in, caught up in his voice, his eyes, hair and face. "Do you believe … dreams … can be real?" I asked, folding my hands in my lap, turning my face his way.

"Yep. I know for a fact dreams come true." He backed out of the parking spot, but he put the Jeep in park and took one of my hands from my lap. I didn't pull away. I couldn't. His fingers, his touch, I knew it in the same way as I knew my own eye color. "You see, Hannah, I had this really weird dream last night. I dreamt about a girl on a stage in a dress and heels with some average guy holding her, singing to her, and I got all sad. I wanted to be the one holding her and singing to her." He pointed at my dress. "She was wearing a dress sort of like yours." He moved his finger up toward my hair. "But she had a sparkly tiara in her hair, with a few springy dark pieces hugging her cheeks, sort of like yours. The same color of hair, at least."

Heat rose to my cheeks.

"I remember snatching her up on stage, staring at her green eyes." He stopped. "Definitely your green, and you want to know why?"

I swallowed. "Why?" I barely asked in a whisper.

"I thought she was in trouble. I thought people were being mean to her." He touched my face. "But you, you don't need saving, do you?"

I found my breath after a long silent pause and sat up straighter. "No, I don't."

Ben leaned away, his eyes full of that familiar pain. In my heart and in every bone in my body, I knew Ben was Gabriel.

"I don't need a boy, either," I said with a smile and grabbed his hand. "And I'm not the type who falls for just anyone."

Ben laughed. "Maybe not. But a guy's got to try, right?"

"Worry about driving us out of here because that fire sounds awesome."

He gave me a sideways smile, making me grin. "As you wish," he said, shifting the Jeep forward.

Mom had once asked me, "*Try to get along with everyone? Please.*" I tried. I thought I could make my way somehow, but the city hadn't been big enough to let me in—instead, it kept me out, which is exactly what I needed.

The tires sliding just a little, Ben blew up a trail of white dust behind us.

Acknowledgements

Dedicated to everyone who has ever had a dream; my friends and family; my niece Hannah, who didn't mind me using her name; and Becky, my best critique partner ever.

I can never say thank you enough to all my friends and family. Your faith and belief in me helped me write every day to become the writer I knew I could be.

Erika Beebe

Inspired by her first grade teacher's belief in her imagination from the first story she ever wrote, Erika has been a storyteller ever since. A dreamer and an experiencer, she envisions the possibilities in life and writes to bring hope when sometimes the moment doesn't always feel that way.

Working in the field of public relations and communications for more than ten years, she has always been involved with writing, editing, and engaging others in public speaking.

Her two young children help keep her creativity alive and the feeling of play in the forefront of her mind.

A Morrow More

Danielle E. Shipley

J. Taylor Publishing

Lorrel lifts his gaze from his writing desk as the autumn breeze and I enter his tent. His glossy black lips smile before his dark brow furrows. "Good morrow," he says. "Word from the commander?"

"Good morrow," I say. "Only this." I step forward to present him a small square of old cloth.

Lorrel folds and sets aside the cloth already on his desktop, the patch I've delivered now taking its place. He opens the desk's shallow drawer, extracts a broad-tipped painter's brush, and removes the tie holding his hair in a knot at the nape of his neck. As he slides the brush through the sleek black waves hanging free just above his shoulders, it takes immense effort on my part not to blatantly gaze.

I have yet to lose my fascination with Inkborn hair.

Or Inkborn movement.

Or the king's part-Inkborn son.

The brush now coated, Lorrel sweeps the bristles back and forth across the face of the cloth before him, and the fabric quickly begins to stain—save, of course, for the sections treated with a solution specially devised to withstand the oils of Inkborn hair. In moments, the once-hidden message is plainly visible, unstained lines forming the words, *The war is over*.

Lorrel lifts his chin, his mouth twitching toward a smile

like the one spreading unchecked across my own face. "This is old news, word-runner." If he means to sound reproving, the twinkle in his eyes spoils the effect.

"And, yet, it is good news," I say, wishing it were my place to throw my arms around him in shared victory, shared relief, shared love.

Standing, he comes around the desk and clasps my hands, my needle-pricked little fingers lost in his strong and sinuous ones. Not the embrace I wish for, but a touch I relish. "Yes, Raeve," he says, voice weighty and warm. "It is good news. Every bit as good this morning as when first delivered two days ago. For a moment, I feared you brought word to contradict it."

I shake my head happily. "The old word stands. The Vale is won. Your company turns toward home tomorrow."

His liquid black eyes search my face. "And what of you?"

"That will depend," I say, my meaning as carefully encrypted as our military's textile code, "on what the Crown may require of me."

"Less of you than of me, perhaps." His gaze drifts past me toward the wind-fluttered tent opening and the castle of Likanstone—a long day's travel beyond. "With more pressing matters now behind us, I expect they shall speak of my marriage again."

I make a noncommittal sound of comprehension. It seems King Cornalis and his wife spoke to their son of little else in the weeks before the beginnings of war demanded their attention almost two years past. The king stood in favor of Lorrel wedding some ally-nation's daughter, while the queen—a whole-blooded Inkborn woman—wished her son to marry a part-Inkblood, like himself. All of it to do with politics I understood little about, until I joined the war effort this spring and, for the first time in my eighteen years, encountered members of the race at the center of all the controversy.

Poor Lorrel has borne a harder time of it than most, being a kingson and a part-blood both. It is fortunate the Inkborn were designed to withstand inhuman pressure.

"Do you know how you will answer them when the time comes?" I ask. Though his parents might push him one way or the other, as he is nineteen, the final say is his own.

"I have known my answer for some time," he says quietly.

My pulse quickens. I wonder, *can he feel it in my hands?* Nothing for it, if he can; I control my breath, but not my blood. Let him feel it. Let him know. Surely he's known before this that I love him.

"Raeve," he says, "I would ask something of you."

"Ask it."

"Will you—"

His lips pause. My breath holds. There's not a sound in my ears but my pounding blood. Even the wind has gone silent.

I wait. My inner tension mounts, but Lorrel is not tense. Only utterly still.

"Yes?" I prompt him. "Will I what? Lorrel?"

He does not answer. He does not move. What's wrong with me that he does not seem to breathe? *Please let it be my eyes*, I beg inside, *don't let it be him, don't let him be*—be what? I don't know what he is, only what he suddenly *isn't*, and whatever this is, I want it stopped. I want him *un*stopped!

"Lorrel, wake up!"

He neither actively restrains, nor releases me, as I pull my hands from his. He does not blink as I wave my hand before his eyes; he does not flinch as I grab his shoulders and shake; he does not respond as I repeat his name—quiet but frantic.

"Lorrel, please. Finish it. Say it! Will I *what?*"

Marry me. I'm sure that's what he'd meant to say, those

words or others with identical meaning. I cannot read his eyes perfectly, but I thought I perceived that much there, and in his voice. I *know* him. Have known him ever since the night I stumbled across him on the far fringes of a field of impromptu battle, since I forced the needle that stood me in good stead as both seamstress and surgeon through the double-dense Inkborn muscle sliced by a foe and felt his enduring strength behind the burning pain as he made hardly a sound.

His silent stillness then was brave and beautiful. Now, it cuts through me like an enemy blade.

"*Why?*" I whisper, eyes narrowed against the threat of tears. *Why* should he live through so much, and still so little, only to stand static in this sudden stop? *Why*, with the war finally over, leaving him free to live and to love in peace and prosperity, is he now held captive? Why is this happening? Come to that, what, exactly, *is* happening?

Nothing so simple as death, surely? He would have fallen by now, not remained upright, his fingers still caressing the space where my hands had been. He stands frozen, yet a touch of my hand to his blue-black cheek confirms his warmth. This is not death, but is it living?

This is beyond my understanding. I must get help.

I walk swiftly from the tent, refusing to burst into a dash for fear I'll likewise burst into a screaming panic. A word-runner of the Crown must maintain her self-control.

Outside, the wind is more than calm; it is as if the air itself holds its breath. Too much of my attention is left behind with the kingson, and as I walk face-first into a leaf, I stifle a startled cry. The leaf hangs in the air, suspended from nothing, slanted in the same direction as the banners atop the soldiers' tents, and the coat billowed around a young officer's legs. *An officer!* I hasten to his side, calling, "Sir, a moment, please!"

No answer. No movement. It is just as with Lorrel. He has halted mid-stride, hand holding a handkerchief halfway to his face, his expression constricted with the warning of a sneeze.

It is the same all throughout the encampment. Men paused in the act of reaching, of pointing, of talking, of laughing. Tears *do* fill my eyes, now, at the sight of a soldier with an arm stopped between an assemblage of laid out belongings and his travel bag. These men were meant to see their homes again tomorrow—some of them for the first time in more than a year. Their families are waiting for them. Or are they?

A new fear wells up inside me. How far has this malady spread?

My tour takes me past the base of the hillock serving as the camp's lookout point, and this inspires a thought. No need to search long for a far-sight glass; one awaits beside the packing soldier's bag. After seizing the instrument with unacknowledged apologies, I return to the hillock's base and up to the top to cast my glass-strengthened gaze out over the Vale.

In the lower reaches, where the winds rarely go, the mists that give the Vaporvale its name shroud the fields, where much of the war has been fought. On the valley's far side, the camp of the enemy stands largely dismantled. The *former* enemy, I remind myself.

According to the terms of their surrender, the last of their soldiers should be gone by sundown. Have they chosen to honor our agreement, or did they make one last play of aggression? Is the frozen state of our camp somehow their doing?

If so, their strange curse has fired backward, as well as to the fore. The view through the far-sight glass shows no more movement, and no less uncanny stillness, across the valley than on my own side.

I lower the glass with trembling hands.

Is all the world frozen? Or is it only the Vale? What of the coastlands beside the Dwindling Sea? What of the world below the waves—the homeland of the Inkborn, before the sun's light and warmth diminished their waters and turned their first source of life stagnant?

I shake my head in pity. Will that poor race know nothing but trouble? It began when their precious Inkwell died, putting an end to the birth of what they called Firstborns—those sprung alive from the black pool below, as opposed to those born from a father and mother. They counted Firstborns a boon, Lorrel told me, for each Inkborn woman's womb can only ever bear a single child, and their people could not otherwise sustain their numbers alone.

With the Inkwell's life gone, they left the sea in search of survival, seeking other people with which to intermarry. Some land-dwellers, such as King Cornalis and his people, have been friends to them; others think them too strange, too far removed from what we call human to be considered as possible mates. That healthy part-bloods, as intelligent and peaceable as the best of either parent race, have been born for decades makes no difference. To those who are determined to think so, to wed an Inkborn is an abomination.

Thus the seeds of war found soil, and each land chose sides as either those who stood by the Inkborn, or those who stood against them. Though reluctant to fight, for most of them value the blood of others nigh as precious as their endangered own, when the Inkborn are resolved to do battle, they do it well. From the moment I witnessed an Inkborn soldier's graceful dance with a sword, I knew our side would win.

Win we did, but this supernatural stillness is not the peace for which we fought.

"What would you do, Lorrel?" I ask aloud. For surely, Lorrel would do *something*, and I am at a loss for ideas.

Go to the top of the world. Clear as if he whispers in my ear, the answer comes.

I stare toward the mountains looming over Likanstone. Though it would be a long shot, and a longer climb, if it's my only chance—if trusting Lorrel means likewise trusting what he trusts—my decision is made.

"True love trusts." With my vow made to the motionless wind, I make my way off the lookout hillock, a short journey down, before I set my sights higher.

There's no telling how long I've walked. Though the distance is easily figured—from the edge of the Vale to the foothills, from there to the mountains proper, and a slow, steep way up—the shadows haven't moved since I left the camp. It ought to have been deep night miles ago, but it is yet morning. Even the sun stands still.

It is not only the world that has frozen. It is time.

Yet, I move.

Why *me*, of all people? I can think of nothing setting me apart as so special. My family is of common stock, and I am but another girl handy with a needle. For a word-runner in wartime, these qualifications were ideal. The enemy may have looked once, but rarely twice, at a plain seamstress wandering in search of clothes to mend in these money-tight times. I stitched rips and patched holes for both sides, theirs and ours—though perhaps the work for them was less meticulously done—and relieved them of rags nobody wanted. Such scraps could always be made into new patches. Or into secret letters slipped up and down chains of command.

All I needed for my task were nimble fingers and a face that appeared honest while guarding the secrets behind it. These I have, and these I gave, but it is no more and far less than others have done. Why should the timeless curse spare me?

Although, in a sense, I *am* cursed—for all I can tell, the most cursed of the lot. Those who hold in their interminable pause may well have no notion of their time's halt. Perhaps for them, in this moment, the moment is all there is. At least if the moment is shared with another, they are not alone. There is no one to share this time outside of time with me.

Unless the word of the Morrow More is true.

On one of those too infrequent nights that found him off-duty, and me in the camp with time to spare after the delivery of a message, Lorrel shared with me the old Inkborn tales—stories of a great being who crafted the world. It seems they left much of the legend behind in the sea, for Lorrel did not know whether Morrow More is its true name or merely the nearest sound his people remember.

"Whatever the name," he said, "the power's the same. The Morrow More rules over all."

He meant this literally, citing the Morrow More's realm as above the highest mountaintop. So in our non-time of trouble, it is there I go.

A single soldier on the march, I combat the too-still silence around me by chanting aloud—the rhythmic repetition of words my only way to mark my private passage of time.

"Through frozen forever, ever I climb,
Higher than the winds do roar,
My quest for the end of the end of time
From the depths of Inkborn lore.
For all that I had, and what's yet to be mine,
Let there be a Morrow More."

But what if the power is gone? asks a doubt within me. *Or frozen, too? Or never was? Or wasn't so great as was thought?*

The Morrow More was thought to be power enough to create the sea, but it's done nothing to keep the waters from dwindling. It was reputed to have fashioned the Inkwell, but the Inkwell did not last. It was supposed to be all that keeps the world running, but the world has stopped! What does that say of the Morrow More?

I pause my climb, unsure anymore of the worth of another step.

My eyes widen as I realize what I've done.

No! I cannot pause! My heart's scream drives me forward. If time has not stopped me, I won't stop myself! Time needs me, *Lorrel* needs me, and I need them both!

I scramble faster, breathing hard, chanting for all I'm worth. "Let there be a Morrow More ... Let there be a Morrow More ... Please, give me my kingson back ... Let us see a morrow more ..."

The food I gathered from the camp never spoils—even that sign of time's passage denied me. It's not the flow of hours, but my own exertion that wearies me. When I close my eyes to rest, it is morning. When I wake from sleep, it is morning. Always the same morning, always the same moment, and still the mountain's summit seems no nearer. I wonder when I shall go mad.

A silly question. There is no 'when'. Not anymore.

"Let us have a morrow more ..." I repeat by rote. "No, let us have an afternoon ... an *evening*." I think with longing of dusky violet skies and crickets. "Let us have a night," I say, remembering stars and moonlight.

"Let us have winter and sparkling snow.
Let us have spring and watch new green grow.
Let us have summer and bask in the glow

Of the sun arching higher and then dipping low.

"Then sunrise," I say, "and autumn again," before turning my gaze back toward the earth left behind me. As I've come so high, it will be pleasant to view the spread of colors along the hills and plains and the edges of the valley. Staring up all this while, I've seen little but blue; perhaps a reminder of red, gold, and green will revive me.

When I look down, however, there is no color. Everything is the white of the floor of the Vaporvale in its mistiest seasons, with lines of darker blurs scattered across. I blink and squint, trying to bring the blurs into focus, hoping to force some glimpse of color through the black and white.

It changes nothing.

"What is become of the world?" With a weary heart but strengthened resolve, I climb on and on—upward and onward—until there is no more mountain to scale.

I stagger to stand upright on the highest plateau, craning my neck to stare into the blank sky still higher. "Great Morrow More, hear me!" I call. "Look down and answer! The world has stopped, and I alone remain to bring you word! I, alone ..." I choke on a sob, feeling more alone than ever.

No answer, no movement. It is the same here as the camp and everywhere. There is no Morrow More, or it is of no help. I am to be alone forever.

Stop crying, I command myself. *Be brave.* Lorrel would be brave. Lorrel would not give up. He would keep trying, keep trusting, if he could. I must be the one to try and trust now.

"Morrow More!" I shout.

Lorrel, I remember, and take courage.

"Morrow More!"

Lorrel.

"Morrow More!"

Lorrel. *Lorrel.*

I've halfway drawn breath to shout again when an enormous face comes into view above like a pale moon in daylight. The vision is hazy and almost transparent, but it is there.

"Somebody calling me?" it asks.

"Yes." My voice croaks. "Yes, I have called to you." I force it louder and firmer. "You *are* the Morrow More, are you not?"

"*The* Morrow More?" the great face asks. Behind the slightly thunderous echo, the voice sounds much like a girl's. "I don't know about '*the*', but yeah, I'm Morrow. How's it going, Raeve?"

I suppose I ought not to be startled that the—that *Morrow* knows my name. If it—or she—is the maker of the world and all people therein, it only makes sense she would.

"It's *not* going," I say. "That's the trouble. Time has stopped!"

Morrow's eyes blink at me through what seem to be a pair of spectacles. "It has? Oh, I'm sorry. I guess that's my fault. It's been a while since I worked on your story."

"My ... story?"

"Yeah, didn't you know? You're living a book. '*Inkborn*' by Morrow More. It's close to finished, I think."

"Finished?" I gasp, my mind a dizzying spin. "What happens when it's finished?"

"I don't know." Morrow's face lowers to rest in her cupped palm, her elbow propped up on some invisible surface. "That's mostly why I haven't been writing, lately. I'm not sure how the story ends."

"And if you don't write what happens next," I say, beginning to understand, "nothing ever will."

"Sounds like," says Morrow, nodding.

"Then you must write!" I cry. "Please, Morrow. You cannot leave the world frozen forever!"

"I can, actually," Morrow says. "I've kind of lost interest in this book. I'm thinking about starting a new one."

I gape in disbelief. "You would abandon this world for another?"

"I don't know. I might. '*Inkborn*' isn't exactly going the way I thought it would. I'd originally planned for it to be, y'know, actually about the Inkborn? At first I tried to write it from Lorrel's perspective, but I was having a hard time getting into his head. That's where you came in," she says, pointing at me. "Your voice showed up really clear, so I shifted more into telling things from your point of view. So now, we've got half the book written one way, the other half written another, and me with no clue how the whole thing resolves. Yay, the Inkborn side wins the war. *Now* what?"

"Now we go home," I say, hoping hard for the statement's truth.

"Okay," Morrow says. "Then what?"

I resist throwing up my hands in exasperation. "Then, I suppose, we live our lives!"

"That's it?" Morrow sounds unimpressed. "'Happily ever after', The End? Kind of anticlimactic."

I cross my arms, working to keep a scowl from claiming my face. "What more would you rather we do?"

Morrow shrugs. "I've been thinking you'd make a cool elf."

My surprise washes all threat of scowling away. "I'd make a what?"

"An elf," Morrow says again. "Elves are one of your standard fantasy races and kind of my early inspiration for the Inkborn before I started taking them in my own direction."

"I do not consider myself to be much like the Inkborn." Though not so dissimilar as their detractors claim, they could never pass for one of my kind, nor I for one of theirs.

"Well, no," Morrow says, "you'd be a different sort of elf spin-off, in a different world. One with winter dragons."

"Winter dragons?" I ask, helplessly.

"Yeah!" Morrow is all excitement. "I thought them up the other day. They're like regular dragons—big, fire-breathing lizards with wings, y'know? Except, instead of fiery hot, winter dragon breath is deadly cold."

I can only listen so long to her oration on the beasts' destructive heat-seeking migration patterns before I raise a hand for silence. "Morrow," I say. "I mean no disrespect. But can you understand why the world of winter dragons might hold less of my interest than otherwise when my *own* world is in great peril?"

"I wouldn't necessarily call it peril," Morrow says, gaze slipping sidelong, no longer meeting mine directly. "I mean, my dropping the book for now or forever wouldn't *harm* anything. It would all just sort of ... fade out, I guess. But *you* wouldn't fade!" she says over my sharp inhalation. "I'd still use you as my heroine, just in another story. You'd probably still keep your name and everything; I like 'Raeve'."

"Forget my name," I say, my voice tight and low to prevent it flying out of control. "Forget me along with everything else you care so little for. I do not wish to go be an elf in your winter dragon book. If you will not write time's continuation, let me freeze, too."

Morrow's face tilts. "I didn't take you for the suicidal type."

"It would hardly be suicide," I say, "because this is not living. To live means to move into the future, moment by moment, not hold still in one breath that never pulls in or blows out. I may be able to move as those below the mountain cannot, but I am nonetheless stuck, for I cannot take the way out you offer."

"Sure you can," Morrow says.

"Lorrel would not."

Morrow regards me with an expression too far and faint to read. "You really are into him, aren't you?" she murmurs. "I didn't plan that either." She purses her lips, eyes considering. "What happens if the story resumes, and he doesn't ask you to marry him?"

I swallow. "Then, I shall live without him. It will be sad." This is not the word I mean. There is no word for what I mean. "But it will be living."

"So you want to go back," she says, "even having no idea whether you'll get a good ending, or not?"

My head cocks in puzzlement. "That's what living is."

"Hmm," she says. "Well, I'll think about it. Later, Raeve."

She's gone without another word.

"Morrow?" I call. "Wait! Morrow More, come back!" I shout and plead, but she does not return.

Now I allow myself to cry, for it is either that or weep against my will. Although I may have lost everything from my future to my only hope, my self-control is yet mine to maintain.

Long after my tears have spent themselves—when my breath has steadied and quieted lower than a whisper, making no sound in the stillness around me—I come to the slow realization that I am left with one thing more.

I make my timeless way back down the mountain, facing the distant black-marked whiteness, which, after my talk with the Morrow More, I now recognize for what it is—a great page of a book, scribbled over with the words that form our unfinished story.

I wonder which of the dark places are words dear to me.

My descent continues beneath the motionless sun. The white ground gradually fades into colors of autumn—the world within the words. I am in no hurry, and I do not tarry, only journey on until, at last, I return to the immobile military camp and step once more into the tent of the kingson.

He is as I left him. Standing straight and elegant, a pace before his writing desk. Gaze of warmest black trained on a point ahead and below. I move forward until that point is my eyes. My hands slip into his gentle hold, and I stare at his mouth poised to shape the word '*you*'.

This is the present our world's writer has left me. I bring my lips to Lorrel's hands, straighten again, and settle in to savor the moment.

"—Deliver one more message for me?" he asks.

My muscles seize. My breath cuts short. I mouth, '*What?*' Months of practice in wartime does little to keep the revelation of astonishment from my face, or of the wary hope building within me.

Lorrel's brows lower. "Are you all right, Raeve?"

Whether I am *all* right, I am too overwhelmed to yet ascertain. Yet, I do not merely dream it; Lorrel is moving, has spoken, is *living* again. For the moment, that is right enough.

"I'm fine," I assure him, working to bring my breathing back into submission. "I'm sorry, what were you saying?" In my excitement over his return to life, I'd missed his words' meaning.

"I have a message for the king," Lorrel says, removing his hands from mine. I would be sorrier for the loss of his touch, were I not so glad to see him capable of motion again.

He turns to the desk and picks up a folded piece of cloth, the one set aside when I delivered the old news of war's end. "I shall return to him morrow after next," he says, "but I would prefer if this word did not wait so long. Will you take it to him?"

"At once, sir," I say, accepting the cloth far easier than accepting that this was all he meant to ask of me. Not marriage, after all. Perhaps I ought to have known better; the Morrow More as good as warned me. Still, I had so very much hoped.

I journey again, reminded every step of the way that, even in my heavy disappointment, this time is better. For this time, time moves.

The autumn breeze dances across my path, partnered now and again with red and golden leaves. Clouds drift across the sky as the sun shifts from morning to noon, and I smile into the light, assured it will sink away in its due hour. People walk the roads and harvest the fields. Birds fly overhead. *Wait. That is no bird.*

Shading my eyes with my hand, I peer intently at the shadowy shape swooping over the distant mountains. Winged like a bird, but far larger, its tail twists behind the creature like a snake's. Or a lizard's.

A dragon, I marvel, as it disappears behind the peaks. How strange. I had been under the impression that this world—this book—contained no dragons. Why else would the Morrow More turn to another story for her winter-breath beasts?

I brighten as a new hope occurs to me. Perhaps the shadow in the sky is a sign of her changed intentions. Rather than uproot me from a forsaken book to be replanted in a new world of elves and winter dragons, she means to bring her other story to me. If so—oh, happy thought! This story is in little danger of being finished any time soon. These creatures will cause pages upon pages of trouble, perhaps greater than the war!

Not that trouble is a good thing, I remind myself, pushing my walking pace a bit quicker. *Still, it is a part of living.* I cannot help but grin.

Having endured an enthusiastic lecture on winter dragons, I understand the danger we face. The king must be warned of

the threat in the mountains. However, there is another word
I must bring him first; Lorrel's message may well be as urgent
as mine.

A deep, beautiful night has fallen when I enter the hall of
Likanstone. King Cornalis and his wife receive me at once, she
running her hairbrush over the cloth so she and her husband
may read the word of their son.

I wait in respectful silence as their eyes scan the letters when,
in an act out of the ordinary, the king hands the cloth back to
me. Upon indication that I am to look it over, I drop my gaze
to the pale lines unstained by Inkborn oil.

To My Lord, King Cornalis, it reads.

*I, Lorrel, kingson, send you greetings from the edge of battle
won, as well as tidings I pray will give both you and my beloved
mother joy. You have desired for some time that I choose whom
I will marry. Thus have I done, and do now make my decision
known to you. With your blessing and her accord, I would marry
she who delivers this word to your hand—courageous servant of
the Crown, dear friend to me in dark times, and possessor of my
heart: My darling, Raeve.*

"Well, word-runner?" asks Cornalis, when I am able to raise
my eyes from the cloth. "Has the kingson your accord?"

Without leave, my face breaks into a broad smile. I almost
wish this moment of pure, delicious joy would last beyond its
rightful measure.

When it doesn't, I am gladder still.

Acknowledgements

To the hope of later, and the joy of now.

In gratitude to my Author for the gift of and passion writing, for the determination to pursue it, and for all of above finally starting to pay off. Remind me that I love yc

A mega thank-you to my writing bestie, Tirzah Duncan, to the whole Stranger Than Truth gang, for letting me ha out with the cool people. Hugs for all of you.

A glass raised high to Jeannie Stine, also one of the cc people, and a treasured helper in the making of this sto Hugs for you, too.

Thanks to Daddy, Momma, Dianne, and Donna, mostly f putting up with me. I may not always make it easy, but sure you think I make it worth it? (Do not answer that.)

A special shout-out to Lute and Will, because there are son people you just have to mention by name, and to Allyn an Edgwyn, who are probably ducking their heads and blushin now. Your time is coming, boys.

Huge thanks to the J. Taylor Publishing team. I will mak it my mission to have you forever looking back on our alli ance with a massive dorky smile and a jittery happy dance, sc we'll be even.

And finally, to everyone who ever gave me encouragement in the midst of discouraging times, bless your hearts like you've blessed mine.

Danielle E. Shipley

Danielle E. Shipley's first novelettes told the everyday misadventures of wacky kids like herself. ...Or so she thought. Unbeknownst to them all, half of her characters were actually closeted elves, dwarves, fairies, or some combination thereof. When it all came to light, Danielle did the sensible thing: Packed up and moved to Fantasy Land, where daily rent is the low, low price of her heart, soul, blood, sweat, tears, firstborn child, sanity, and words; lots of them. She's also been known to spend short bursts of time in the real-life Chicago area with the parents who homeschooled her and the two little sisters who keep her humble. When she's not living the highs and lows of writing young adult novels, she's probably blogging about it.

Made in the USA
Lexington, KY
16 December 2013